I0763520

Candy Striper

Veronica Henderson

Candy Striper

Veronica Henderson

Copyright © 2024 by Veronica Henderson.

All rights reserved.

No part of this book may be reproduced or transmitted in any form or by any means, electronic or mechanical, including photocopying, recording, or by any information storage and retrieval system, without permission in writing from the copyright author, except for the use of brief quotations in a book review.

ISBN: 978-1-63960-030-4 Paperback
978-1-63960-031-1 Hardcover
978-1-63960-032-8 E-book

Published in the United States by Pen2Pad Ink Publishing.

Requests to publish work from this book or to contact the author should be sent to: mrsrhonie@aol.com

Veronica Henderson retains the rights to all images.

Table of Contents

In the world of home health, Vera Henson thrived—her days filled with purpose and compassion. But one fateful day, everything changed. A single event shook the foundation of her beliefs, leaving her questioning the very core of her existence. Will things ever return to normal, or has the fabric of her carefully crafted life been irreversibly altered?

As Vera grapples with doubt and uncertainty, the looming question lingers: Was she truly doing a great job, or had she been missing something crucial all along? Only God knows the answers in this gripping tale of self-discovery, resilience, and the unwavering pursuit of purpose.

Welcome to 'The Candy Striper,' where the lines between the familiar and the unknown blur, and Vera Henson's journey takes an unexpected turn into the heart of the human experience.

Chapter 1

How It All Started

I slowly hung up the phone. I have made this phone call many times before and the answer has always been the same, "We don't need any help. We will call you just as soon as we get an opening," but I haven't received a call yet. I was fourteen years old, and I felt like I was ready to work. Then all of a sudden, the telephone rang. I got excited thinking maybe that was them calling me right back, but it wasn't. I answered the phone, "Hi, this is Vera." It was a call from the Sunday School teacher. She was calling to give me the name and number of an older female adult in the neighborhood that needed some assistance.

I always carried my green steno pad with me because it was good for taking notes. I took down all of the information and I thanked her for the new referral. Now I was really excited. I may have a new client. I already had two clients in the neighborhood, but I would just go by and pick up the grocery list and walk to the corner market to pick up the items they needed, deliver them, and take the time to place them on the shelves where they belong. I also loosened all of the tops on the jars or whatever they needed because most of my clients didn't have the grip power to open jars. So business was picking up and I was getting excited about that.

Mrs. Genevive Savage lived about three blocks from my home in South Memphis. I walk past the street every morning on my way to school. Her voice sounded very young on the phone. It didn't sound like the voice of an eighty-year-old woman. We talked on the phone for nearly an hour, and she remembered me from church, but I couldn't remember her. I sang in the choir for several years and was also on the junior usher board. Maybe when I see her, I will remember her face. Mrs. Savage had a niece that lives with her and had been her primary caregiver since her husband had passed away fourteen months ago. Her niece, Miss Karen Savage was a rising star real estate agent in Memphis. I had seen her pictures on posters, different advertisements on something or another. Maybe I will get the opportunity to meet her also.

Mrs. Savage was unable to walk and could not open the door for me when I arrived the following Saturday. There were strict instructions to ring the doorbell and to come around to the right window on the left side of the house. My mom did not like these instructions at all, so she drove me to my first visit with Mrs. Savage. Mom waited until I gained entrance inside the home. If everything was okay, I was to return to the front door and wave the okay sign with my hand in sign language. Mom will not leave until I give her the signal. I rang the doorbell and then I proceeded to the window.

I could hear Mrs. Savage asking who was at the door. I yelled in my booming voice, "Hi, this is Vera Williams." She leaned forward and I could barely see her face, but she could see me through that window pretty good. What happened next was surprising. A long, red, broom-like stick was coming through a round hole in the window casing, where I was standing. The stick nearly poked me in the eye. It has a key professionally attached to the end. This was the key that I needed to use to let myself into the home of Mrs. Savage.

As I reached the front door, I held the red pole in one hand and gave mom the okay sign with my other hand for her to move along. I unlocked the front door, and I entered the home of my new client, Mrs. Savage. I noticed that mom still hadn't driven away, and I would be willing to bet that she remained parked several minutes outside longer before she pulled away. The home was very spacious and very clean. On my way to the left rear side of the house, I passed by a piano and several large plants and a lot of oil paintings on the wall. It was just beautiful.

I immediately handed Mrs. Savage her door key. I took a good look at her face, and I didn't remember her. We talked for some time, and I could tell that she needed companionship and someone to talk to. She stated she was blind in one eye and did not share which eye had the problem. She was also hard of hearing because I had to keep my voice elevated the whole time that I was there. Mrs. Savage was unable to walk due to a stroke that she had several years ago. I also noticed that she had a catheter.

She gave me instructions on how to prepare her lunch. Her lunch was easy to prepare. Most older adults usually eat the same dish about three times a week. The favorite pick for Mrs. Savage was a can of Sweet Sue Chicken & Dumplings with crackers. I was not much of a cook. I was a baker, but I knew how to make any dish appealing. After heating the dumplings on the stove and placing them in a nice bowl, I decorated the rest of the plate with a lot of crackers. Mrs. Savage also requested a large glass of Diet Sprite to be served with her meals at all times. I made sure that I was cleaning the kitchen as I went. I took her meal to her. As she was eating, I started to water all of the plants in her house according to her instructions.

Later, I emptied the catheter bag and made sure to secure the safety lock on it. Mrs. Savage stated that if the bag is not closed properly, the urine is guaranteed to spill out on the floor. Since I did not want to be mopping urine, I made sure that the lock was secure on the bag. I sat on the chair right beside her bed so I could see out of the window. I knew that it would be dark in a few hours, but Mrs. Savage talked for about another hour or so. I was happy to entertain her. We had a good conversation. I learned that she played the piano at churches and a lot of private functions. She also painted all of the paintings in her home. Her husband was her primary caregiver until he passed away from natural causes. Her niece, Karen, spends almost every night with her. It appeared to me that she was alone most of the time during the day.

Mrs. Savage was very pleased with my work and asked if I was available from noon until 4:00 PM. I was happy to be available. I had the feeling that I was the luckiest girl in the world. I was making my own money and life was good. On my way out, I made sure to close all of the blinds, turn on the porch light, and make sure that the front door was locked and secure - all that was requested by Mrs. Savage.

It took me about twenty minutes to walk home. I had to be home before dark. This was one of the most important of mom's house rules so there was no lolly-gagging today. Not to mention that she would be looking forward to hearing all about my day with Mrs. Savage. Everything was pretty much written in my green little notepad. I didn't want to skip a beat. Mom always enjoyed my adventures and my activities with my clients. She could hardly wait for me to get home so she could hear everything. It gave her an opportunity to take a break from making designer wedding gowns, bridesmaid dresses and a ton of choir robes for the local churches.

I had the pleasure of working with Mrs. Savage for several more weeks. Around the fourth weekend, she asked me to do her a huge favor. I told her that I think that I could make that happen. It didn't seem like a big deal, but I would need some transportation. Before arriving at Mrs. Savage's house, I had to stop at the neighborhood malt stand. I took my bike out of the storage shed and drove in the opposite direction to the malt stand. I ordered a large strawberry milkshake for Mrs. Savage. I got back on my bike and drove a block past my home and even faster to get to Mrs. Savage's home because I didn't want that milkshake to melt.

The milkshake was still cold, and I arrived safely. I pulled my bike right up to the front door and rang the doorbell. I was afraid to leave my bike unattended for any amount of time, so I ran around to the side of the house to retrieve the door key from the side window and let myself in. I had the milkshake in one hand, the key pole was under my armpit, and I pulled my bike through the door with my other hand. Mrs. Savage never left her bedroom and therefore she would never know that I parked my bike in her kitchen. I could hear Mrs. Savage from the back bedroom asking, "Did you bring it? Did you bring the milkshake?" I guess I didn't respond back quickly enough for her because I was out of breath. I caught my breath; I gave her the milkshake and returned the door key to Mrs. Savage. She didn't talk much that day. She was sipping on that milkshake all day long with this big smile on her face. It was priceless. So I started watering the plants and did a little dusting. I even went outside to get the mail. The mailbox was full.

Upon returning, I placed all of the mail on the nightstand near Mrs. Savage's bed. She has a special silver tray on which she likes to have the mail stored. I proceeded to the kitchen to prepare her lunch, and I almost knocked over my bike. I slowly moved the bike to the front door. The lunch menu for Mrs. Savage never changed. It was always the same. I wasn't sure that she could eat her lunch along with drinking that large milkshake, and a large Diet Sprite. I prepared the lunch as usual and twenty-seven minutes later, the answer was yes. She ate everything on the menu.

Mrs. Savage asked me to take out the trash that day, especially the cup that contained the large milkshake. Now this was a mystery, but I didn't ask any questions. I always took out the trash before leaving. Maybe I was missing something. I made notes in my little notepad. As I was leaving for the day, Mrs. Savage paid me my wages for the day, and she also gave me extra money for the milkshake - that was $1.00, and she told me to keep the change.

The following Saturday when I went to visit Mrs. Savage was very peculiar. After ringing the doorbell and introducing myself as always, it took a long time for Mrs. Savage to pass the key through the window. I retrieved the door key as usual and let myself in. I hurried to Mrs. Savage's bedroom as always. She was happy to see me. I asked, "How are you doing today?" She stated that she was not feeling well. I returned the key and asked if there was anything that I could do to make her feel better. She stated, "I am much better now that you have arrived."

Mrs. Savage was always kind to me, and she always had a great spirit, but today something was off. We started the day off by addressing some get-well cards to some of her friends. I didn't think that she had any friends because I never saw any visitors and the telephone hardly ever rang. But what do I know? She already had the cards picked out and her address book on her bed beside her. We got our mission accomplished that day. We addressed the cards, and she made little notes. We got the cards sealed and applied the postage stamps. I even gathered them up and took them to the mailbox before the postman came.

I later went to the kitchen to prepare

Mrs. Savage's lunch. She usually has lunch on Saturdays around noon when I come to visit. Today I was running behind on our normal schedule. After going into the pantry to retrieve the can of dumplings, I noticed a card with my name on it. The handwriting on the envelope didn't belong to Mrs. Savage. I took notice of her handwriting from the address book and also of her signing of the get-well cards. I didn't open the envelope right away, but I did continue to prepare her lunch as usual. After serving Mrs. Savage her lunch, I returned to the kitchen to read the contents of the envelope that was addressed to me. The message was from Mrs. Savage's niece, and it was simple and direct to the point.

Hi Vera,

Please don't bring any more milkshakes of any kind to my aunt. She is diabetic and lactose intolerant. When I arrived home last Saturday, Mrs. Savage was lying in bed covered in feces and too weak to call for help. Her sugar level was elevated through the roof, and it took me two hours to get her bathed, get the sheets changed and everything under control. Now remember Vera, no more milkshakes of any kind outside of the food that is located in the kitchen. Thank you very much.

Karen Savage

Hmm, the mystery has been solved. I could have disposed of the empty milkshake cup, but the outcome would have been the same. Some older adults would eat things that would make them sick. I have to make a note of that. Mrs. Savage has a special diet. No milkshakes allowed and no outside food. I didn't discuss the note with Mrs. Savage, and I finished tidying up the kitchen after lunch. I developed a bad feeling in the pit of my stomach. Maybe I was getting in over my head. I didn't want to serve any type of food that would harm them or cause them enough damage that it would take their life. I could see the headlines now in the Memphis Newspaper, *"Fourteen-year-old serves milkshake to senior causing death."* I know - I am over exaggerating.

I said my goodbyes to Mrs. Savage after I completed all of my chores. I told her that I would see her next Saturday at the same time. She was very happy about that, and I knew that she would be. We enjoyed each other's company so much. Before I left, I placed a note on the kitchen counter for Karen Savage. I took a piece of paper from my green notepad.

Dear Miss Karen Savage,

Thank you for the update. I am so sorry for the inconvenience, and it will not happen again.

Vera Williams

I walked to the front door, flipped the switch to turn the porch light on as usual, secured the front door and started to walk home. It started to rain but I barely noticed. I simply put one foot in front of the other while silently praying as I made it to my home. It never dawned on me not even for one minute that I would never see Mrs. Genevieve Savage again. She passed away the following Thursday night at Baptist Hospital.

Miss Karen was nice enough to call and talk to Mom. It was Mom who had to deliver the sad news to me. Death was not a stranger to me for I had seen it many times. I had ushered at the church for many funerals, and I also attended my father's funeral as well. Many times I had wondered if the milkshake really had anything to do with her dying, and then I would ask myself if I would do it again. With tears rolling down my face, if the truth be told, there was a great possibility that I would honor the request and get that milkshake.

Chapter 2

Private Duty Sitting

Several years later, I married my high school sweetheart, Marcus Henson, several weeks after my high school graduation. We really didn't have anything in common, but he was my friend and we both loved old school music. We would spend many days listening to The Commodores, Maze or The Isley Brothers. I loved to hear Marcus sing. A year into our marriage, we welcomed our son Melvin Henson - 8 pounds. Two years after that we welcomed our daughter Simone - 9 pounds. Wow! I am twenty-one years old with two children who I loved dearly. Marcus and I had talked about having four to six children, but those labor pains changed my mind very quickly. I loved being a mom, but I had to work. I needed to be responsible for my share of the bills.

Our budget demanded two full-time workers. I wasn't caring for as many people as I was when I was younger and needed to boost my business, so I had to get creative. I ran an ad in the local newspaper. The ad was only supposed to run two Sundays in a row because most people in Memphis took the Sunday paper and not the daily paper. The ad in the paper was ran like this,

Please don't put Mom or Dad in the nursing home. Call Vera Henson at 901-562-2781.

I was excited. It was short, didn't cost a lot of money and was hoping to get some really good clients from that ad. The first call I received was from a nursing home.

"Hi. This is Harmony Village Nursing Home. We do not appreciate you putting an ad in the paper asking people to call you. We're a great nursing home. Would you please take down the ad? It gives nursing homes a bad rep."

I said, "Thank you for the information," and hung up the phone. Well, that didn't make me feel good. The second call I received was from a young lady named Patty wanting me to provide her name and telephone number of all of my overflow. Patty told me that I couldn't take care of all the people, and I could just easily give her the name and number, and she would contact any overflow that I had or if I had too many clients to take care of. That didn't go over well with me at all because I didn't know Patty. If I was going to recommend someone for a position, I sure would like to know what their work ethics were like.

The third call I received was very promising. It was from a ninety-two-year-old woman by the name of Mrs. Nancy Logan. I was interviewed over the phone.

"Hello, may I speak with Mrs. Vera Henson please?"

"Hello, this is Vera. How may I help you?" I asked.

"My name is Nancy Logan. I saw your ad in the paper, and I need a sitter with my disabled husband that I am caring for. How long have you been a caregiver?"

"Over 10 years now."

"Are you certified, and do you have relevant licenses or credentials?"

"I am not a certified nursing assistant, but that is my ultimate goal."

"I would love to assist you."

"Does he have any chronic medical conditions I should be aware of?", I asked.

"Well he is nonverbal."

"Are there any recent surgeries or hospitalizations I need to know about?"

"No ma'am."

"What is his current mobility like?"

"Mr. Logan is bedridden and almost completely nonverbal", she replied.

We stayed on the phone for about 30 minutes asking questions back and forth before I accepted the position. This would be my first male client. Mrs. Logan needed someone to work Thursday through Sunday six hours a day from the hours of 9:00 AM to 3:00 PM. I worked out the babysitting schedule between Mom and Marcus. Mom always enjoyed the kids visiting and Marcus was off every weekend. I thank God every day that Mom only lived two blocks away. She was always there when I needed her.

I dropped the kids off the following Thursday, and I arrived at the Logans at 8:50 AM sharp. I rang the doorbell and knocked on the door for what seemed like forever. Then a small framed, short elderly woman answered the door. "Come on in Vera", she replied. Mrs. Logan escorted me directly to Mr. Logan's room and I was not prepared for Mr. Logan. Mr. Logan was tall. His body was as long as the hospital bed, but his skin was as white as a ghost. He was bedridden and unable to talk. When he opened his mouth, only an *"Aaaahhhh"* sound would escape through his lips. The sound would make the hairs stand up on the back of my neck. Mrs. Logan started yelling, "Calm down Lewis. Calm down." The more she tried to calm him down, the louder he squealed.

The doorbell rang and someone was knocking at the door. The Logans couldn't hear a thing. It was my opportunity to leave all that chaos for a minute and go answer the door. As soon as I opened the door, a female in uniform introduced herself as Barbara. She speedily stepped inside and went into the chaos in that room. Now it was the four of us in the room and the action continued. Barbara was the home help aide who came out three times a week to give Mr. Logan a bed bath. I, on the other hand, was the sitter.

I observed everything that Barbara did. Mrs. Logan left the room. Barbara washed her hands and put on a pair of gloves. Barbara was a professional. She borrowed Mr. Logan's bedside table and placed towels, liquid soap, deodorant, lotion, and a large square tub of water on it. She swiftly began to wash Mr. Logan. She washed Mr. Logan's face, his neck, both arms and all of the front upper torso. Then she towel dried him and applied lotion. She had a system and it appeared to be a good one.

Barbara loved her work and she also loved to talk. She stated that she had been a home health aide for twelve years, raised three kids as a single mom and she enjoys camping and fishing in her spare time. Mr. Logan appears to be enjoying his bath. It was very quiet. The more she worked with him, the calmer he became. As Barbara washed his back, she gently applied the lotion with a massage-like technique. Mr. Logan was completely quiet but not asleep. She completed the bath with care, changing the linen on the bed and also changing the adult diapers that Mr. Logan wore. Barbara used a lift to raise Mr. Logan up in the air while she changed the sheets on the bed. The lift was also used to bring Mr. Logan down easily and safely back onto the bed. Barbara completed the bed bath in forty-five minutes without a sweat.

Mrs. Logan signed the paperwork for Barbara, and she left. I was alone with Mr. Logan for the moment. He was finally asleep. I was studying the lift that Barbara used. The lift came with a large pad which was placed under Mr. Logan. She would roll him to one side and roll him to the other side all the while pushing the pad evenly under his body. The lift was made out of steel and had a pair of chains. Each chain had two hooks on each end. The hooks latch on to the four hooks on the pad. There was also some type of steel on each side of the pad which made a firm grip once the hooks were connected. Once everything was connected then you would use a large handle on the side of the handle and pump it up and down like pumping water out of the well in the old days.

I took mental note of all of this. I stayed in the recliner in Mr. Logan's room and made notes of everything that was taking place, all the activity, all the chaos. I also made notes step by step of the proper way to give a bed bath to a bedridden male. I also took notes of learning how to use the hydraulic patient body lift as well as tube feeding and changing adult diapers on a male. My lord! That was a lot for a private duty sitter, but I was eager and ready. I worked for the Logans for almost a year, and I had the pleasure of meeting Barbara on many occasions.

I liked Barbara. She was an excellent worker and a great teacher. I gained experience in learning a lot of different techniques for working with the Logans. I even learned how to become successful at tube feeding - adding water before and after each feeding. I think the greatest task I learned was when Mr. Logan had a bowel movement. I learned how to change those adult diapers. Thanks to Barbara, I became really good at it.

The Logans often have company. Mrs. Logan would love to dress up. They didn't have any children so that's why I am assuming she looked forward to the mothers of the church coming to visit her. Whenever Mrs. Logan had company, she introduced me as the sitter - not Vera - but the sitter. After this happened on several occasions, I decided to enroll at Rice College and completed the Nursing Assistant program. I graduated at the top of my class. It was so hard to juggle the classes, a husband, two kids, church activities and the Logans. One thing that I was grateful for was the opportunity to be able to study while I was at the Logans. During the quiet time, I could go over many chapters, and I was thankful for that. Look at what God can do. I did it! Vera Henson - certified nursing assistant.

Several weeks later on my visit to the Logans, I was standing outside getting ready to knock at the front door. A foul smell tore into my nostrils and I nearly fainted. Before I could knock, I could hear

Mr. Logan squealing loudly and once inside, I could see poop meeting me at the front door. Something similar to this had happened before per Barbara. Mrs. Logan was shouting at me to the top of her voice, "Well come on in Vera! You got a lot of work to do today. Let's get everything done and cleaned up before my company arrives." She was expecting company from the church today. I politely asked Mrs. Logan to please take off her shoes because she was tracking poop all over the house. I placed newspapers on the carpet, in the bedroom, in the living room, in the dining room, and everywhere Mrs. Logan has tracked poop. I placed plenty of newspapers in Mr. Logan's room. I gave him a bed bath, and I changed the sheets on his bed. I cleaned poop which seemed like for days.

The lift was good for lifting Mr. Logan, but that day I decided not to use the lift because I knew that it would not bode well on top of the newspaper. This made my job just a little bit harder, but I could do it. After bathing Mr. Logan, I put all of the dirty items into the washer, and I hit the start button after adding the detergent. Later, I got out the mop bucket, added Pine-Sol and hot water and I proceeded to mop the carpet. I started at the front door mopping the carpet. I mopped carpet for over 60% of the house that day. I had to change the mop water twice. I turned on all of the ceiling fans to assist with drying the carpet. At last, my nose was no longer burning. Mr. Logan was finally quiet, and I needed him to rest so that I could take a break.

I disposed of the trash by removing all the soiled newspapers, carrying it through the den door. While doing so, I noticed the trash can had tipped over, leading me to gather the spilled items. Among them were numerous empty containers of liquid stool softener, laxative, and anti-diarrhea medicine. Carefully placing everything, including other trash, into the can, I put the lid on very tightly. Now I know what Mrs. Logan has been putting into her husband's feeding tube, causing his distress. This has to be the reason why he squeals so much. I had to pray about this for a while. I figured out how I could help Mr. Logan. I waited until my next visit when Barbara would be present.

I wrote a note detailing the situation and shared it with her. Barbara read the note and assured me she would take care of it. She said she would pass the information to her supervisor for investigation. This intervention alleviated my concern about

Mrs. Logan potentially administering over-the-counter laxatives to Mr. Logan without proper oversight.

I didn't know what the chain of command was in reporting Mrs. Logan. I wasn't even sure if it was something to be reported, but I felt in my spirit that this was not right. I talked it over with Marcus. We decided that maybe I had spent enough time at the Logan's, and it was time for me to move on to find new clients.

So the next time I went to the Logan's, I knew that it would be my last visit. I sat down and discussed with Mrs. Logan that this would be my last visit. She was not happy with that at all. As a matter of fact, I think the whole day went to hell in a handbasket. I guess I had seen a side of Mrs. Logan that I had never seen before. I went in the room and took care of Mr. Logan. I gave him his bath, and the day was going pretty good. Halfway through the shift, Mrs. Logan walked in and told me that I was fired. It wasn't a surprise to me for some reason.

Anyway, I gathered my things, told Mr. Logan goodbye, prepared to leave but someone was knocking at the door. Mrs. Logan looked at me and told me, "Hold on Vera. Just hold on a minute." Now it's peculiar that of all days she could hear someone knocking at the door because most times Mrs. Logan doesn't hear the doorbell or anybody knocking on the door. She goes to the door and opens it. It's an unexpected visitor dropping off a couple of pies. She lets her visitor in and I am standing in the hallway with my bag and notepad ready to walk out of the door. Mrs. Logan, for the first time, introduced me as Vera, the private duty sitter. I, on the other hand, introduced myself to her visitor as Vera Henson, a new graduate from Rice College as a certified nursing assistant.

I thanked Mrs. Logan for allowing me to work for her and proceeded to walk out the door. I never visited the Logan's household again. For a couple of weeks after the last visit, my phone did ring. Mrs. Logan had decided to hire me back, and I decided not to take the position.

Chapter 3

The Accident

It was late March of 2003. The weather in Memphis was still cool and crisp just the way I like it. It was a beautiful morning, and I was looking forward to a blessed day. Today I decided to wear my new uniform. It was a chocolate brown scrub dress that ran about 6 inches below my knee with a matching jacket. I'm excited to wear it because it was custom made with a built-in back brace to give me the support I need while working with my clients each day.

The neighbor's dog was barking early this morning. We didn't really need an alarm clock because you could hear the dogs barking daily at 6:00 AM, 10:00 AM, 2:00 PM and so on every four hours until midnight. My neighbor, Jennifer, had eight German Shepherds who were mostly inside dogs, and they were her little fur babies. On the other hand I am allergic to them and very afraid of them. I also have asthma and haven't had an attack in years. As long as Jennifer and her fur babies stayed on her side of the fence we were good.

The kids were almost dressed for school. Simone was two years younger than Melvin, but they were as different as orange and black. Melvin, my oldest, was in high school and he was just learning how to drive. I was his part time driving instructor. Later today we will go out and do some practice driving. I was waiting on my better half, Marcus, to volunteer to assist with the driving lessons...I'm still waiting.

I shuttle the kids to separate schools every morning, unaware of Marcus's mysterious comings and goings due to our carpooling arrangement. Ensuring the kids make it to school in time for breakfast is just the tip of the iceberg; handing them lunch money is routine, but Simone's insatiable need for extra cash, likely for school supplies, raises suspicion. Truth be told, I think she's buying snacks instead. In which I will add that to my list of things I need to investigate later.

As Vera Henson, a seasoned caregiver with over seventeen years of experience, my journey has seen various titles—home health aide, nursing assistant, private duty sitter—yet, at the core, we're all caregivers. The roots of my passion go back to my dad's wise words: find something you love enough to do for free. For me, that something has always been caregiving!

It's 8:30 AM and I'm sitting in McDonald's parking lot finishing my breakfast. I ordered the same thing every morning. A large sweet tea, one sausage biscuit sandwich and one packet of jelly. Then I drove to my next destination. I parked my aging gold Lincoln Continental in the driveway of my first client's home, Mr. Brown.

He's been a client of mine for several years. I assist him with caring for his wife Lola Brown who is unable to do anything for herself. She is close to eighty years old, bed ridden, and mostly nonverbal. Mr. Brown is her primary caregiver. They don't have any children or family members that can help. Together we proceed to give her a bed bath, comb, brush, and braid her hair, and change the linen on her bed. Mrs. Brown weighed about 150 pounds and her hair was at least twenty-four inches long. The door was always open when I arrived on Mondays, Wednesdays, and Fridays. I let myself in as usual and put my tote bag in the chair in the den. Then greeted the Browns in the main bedroom.

"Good Morning Mr. and Mrs. Brown," I said. He greets me with a smile as usual.

"Good Morning Vera. I'm so glad to see you and have some help."

"Well let me get prepared and we can get started."

I went to the bathroom to wash my hands, put on my gloves, and got ready to get my day started with Mrs. Brown. Mr. Brown has a stern routine that we must follow precisely at each visit. He will proceed to wash her body with a ton of soap and water. My job is to rinse, dry and apply lotion to each and every part of her body, to keep up with him and to never lose the rhythm. He changes the water in the bathing bin at least three to four times during each procedure because she likes hot water. I usually take this time to catch my breath. Together we work as a team. Of course, Mr. Brown is the team leader.

After bathing Mrs. Brown, changing the sheets and pillowcases on the bed, it's now time to brush her hair. It's still black, a good grade, with a little bit of gray. If Mr. Brown could count all the strands of hair on her head; he would surely do so in a heartbeat. I began slowly combing and brushing her hair. According to Mr. Brown the brushing of the hair has to be at least fifty strokes, so I make sure to count as I go. This procedure takes up to twenty minutes, sometimes longer to complete and his eyes are on you. I pray silently that he would need to excuse himself for one reason or another, but it never happens.

After combing and brushing her hair into one long braid, here comes the most important part of the whole procedure: every piece of her hair in the comb and brush, the flooring, my clothes, the bed, or anywhere must be placed on the white towel and given to Mr. Brown. He'll always make sure that this procedure is done correctly. Why? Because he has to burn her hair. The reason he burns the hair is so that the birds will not gain possession of Mrs. Brown's hair and use it to make a bird's nest. He has explained this many times, but I still scratch my head about that one.

I asked him why this ritual was so important. He said, "If the birds get a hold to the hair and build a nest with it, then she will scratch her head like crazy." Now of course, that is the craziest thing that I ever heard, but being in the business for as long as I have you will hear many things. Even now I can get a surprise every now and again.

I only saw two clients that day and it was Wednesday. I always liked to prepare a special meal for my family on Wednesday evenings. We always got together and had a breakfast buffet at home. We would have a feast that consisted of bacon, biscuits, and pancakes. Also included were scrambled eggs, smothered potatoes with onions, sausage, and some type of fruit. This was my way of apologizing to my family for not preparing breakfast throughout the week. I had already stopped at the store on the way home to pick up fresh eggs and juice along with some other items I needed.

I called home and Melvin answered the phone. I asked him to meet me in the driveway in ten minutes to assist me with getting the groceries out of the car. The Memphis traffic was terrible around five o'clock in the evening. We lived on one of the busiest streets in town, but I had finally made it home. I could see Melvin standing on the porch and he was excited just waiting for me to pull into the driveway. I had the left signal light flashing, but I had to be patient in making the turn safely. All of a sudden, something hit the back of my car. I was sitting there in shock thinking, *"I just got hit!"* I looked around and saw that two of the fresh eggs in the back seat were now in the front with me all crushed up. The next thing I heard was someone tapping on the window. I rolled the window down and there was a young man standing there not much older than my son. He was crying and very upset.

"Ma'am, I just hit you! Are you okay?" He said.

"I..." I started to speak.

"I need you to get out and take a look at your car." He continued.

"I'm okay...I'm fine I think." I responded.

I got out of the car, walked to the back and stood between the cars to see how much damage had been done. I didn't see a whole lot of damage on my car. My Lincoln was still standing strong. I decided to look at his vehicle when all of a sudden out of the corner of my eye I saw the young man jump backward. When I awakened a short time later, I realized I was under a vehicle and could see fluid leaking around me. Confused and in a daze, I could hear a calming voice around me saying, "I got this." "What do you have?" I replied, and the voice replied again, "I got this." This discussion went on for quite some time. As

I looked around, I couldn't see anybody else lying in the street but me.

A short time later, two pairs of hands grabbed the bottom of my dress and gently pulled me out from under the front wheels. I recognized the hands to the right of me as they were my son Melvin's. The other set of hands were from a stranger. My adrenaline was high, and my breathing was not normal. I could feel my heartbeat pumping loudly inside my ears and my eyesight was blurry. I noticed that I wasn't even wearing my glasses. I didn't know where my glasses were.

"What's going on?", I said. There was a large crowd of people standing around me and I knew that something was up. I saw Melvin standing very close to me in a semi-leaning position, a little too close if you ask me. The expression on my face was like a page out of a book. I knew that Melvin was hiding something. I raised my head up just a little, and I could see that my right leg was broken. My bones were exposed but the black thigh high hosiery that I had on acted as a support bandage and kind of kept things together. That was me lying in the street wondering what was happening next. Where is the young man that accidentally hit my car? I don't see him anywhere.

There was blood on my hands, mostly on my knuckles. My hands started searching other parts of my body for damages. I touched my face and there was more blood on the left side of my forehead. It was swollen tremendously. As I was searching, I was taking mental notes. There was a feeling in my left thigh but not my right. I could move both of my arms with no pain. I took another quick assessment of my damaged right leg and it looked really bad. I thought to myself, "I may lose this leg. It may have to be replaced."

An ambulance had finally arrived to take me to the hospital. I knew that my body needed to get out of the street and into the ambulance. That means that the paramedics had to move me. Afraid that the transition would be extremely painful I closed my eyes really tight to prepare myself for the movement. I could hear the voices of many people talking around me. All of a sudden, I felt my body being lifted and placed onto something much softer than the street.

At that moment, I was overwhelmed with thoughts and emotions. I felt like my life was going to change forever because I wouldn't be me anymore. I didn't think that anyone would be concerned with my feelings and this new life I would have to figure out would only be important to me. As my mind raced with thoughts they were interrupted by a small voice:

“Your name and date of birth...Can I have your name and date of birth please?”

“Vera Henson, August 26, 1960.” I answered with my eyes still closed.

My blood pressure was taken, doors were closed loudly, and the vehicle drove away with such speed I felt as if I was running from the police. The fast ride did not last long. Upon arrival at the emergency room, things were moving faster than me and the ride to get there. My blood pressure was taken again, and I was asked the same questions as before. “What is your name? What is your birthdate?” Although I knew it was necessary at that moment, I didn’t want anyone to ask me anything else. I was ready to ask the nurse if she had a pen and paper so I could write down the answers to the questions and lay them on my chest to avoid repeating it over and over again. Then I was asked to open my eyes. Still scared I did so but only for a short time. I needed to keep my fear level at a minimum.

An IV was successfully placed in my left arm when the nurse stated,

"We need to prepare you for surgery."

"Surgery?!?!"

"Yes ma'am on your right leg immediately." Just then my fear level had elevated to the max.

"We are removing your clothes."

I have been in the medical field for many years, so I understood that when you go to the hospital, you have to take off all your clothes in exchange for a hospital gown that exposes all of your buttocks. I was familiar with the procedure. One nurse gave me something for pain through the IV while another nurse took care of business slowly by cutting my beautiful brown uniform with the matching lab jacket away from my body. I could tell that she was a professional and that she really enjoyed her job. She started cutting at the hem of my dress on one side. She sliced right through the dress, through the jacket, through the underwear and through my bra. She moved over to the other side and did the same exact thing.

Whatever medicine that was inserted into my IV, it took all of my fighting power. I had to go to the restroom, and I was hungry, but it felt as if all of a sudden my body had forgotten. I couldn't feel anything. The nurse and her assistant gently rolled me to one side and pulled away every stitch of my clothing from my body and placed those items in some bags.

“How much do you weigh?” Someone asked me.

“Head trauma” I heard someone else say.

“Combined tibia and fibula fracture” another voice called out.

“Obesity” another voice shouted.

Those were the last words I could vaguely hear as I began to drift away while being wheeled from emergency into surgery. When I came to, I was greeted by a nurse.

“Hello Mrs. Henson, my name is Maria, and I will be your nurse today while you are in the recovery room. Please tell me your date of birth...”

“August 26, 1960” I answered groggily.

“Thank you! Your surgery lasted two and a half hours but everything went well.” Maria went on to take my blood pressure, body temperature, pulse rate and respiratory rate all manually.

“Are you in any pain?”

"No."

"Do you need anything?"

"No" I responded again.

Maria had a gentle quiet voice. The kind of voice she had made you feel safe, and right now feeling safe was exactly what I needed. A short time later I was transferred to my room on the fourth floor. The young man who pushed my bed down the long hallway all the way to the elevator never said a word to me. I was asleep by the time I arrived at my room but was awakened not too long after by someone requesting to draw blood. I wish I had my glasses because I wanted to know what she was doing and just how many tubes of blood were being taken from my body. The blood samples were withdrawn, and the phlebotomist disappeared in a flash. I was in a private room, and I thank God so much for that. I was still groggy from the anesthesia.

Darkness had fallen outside the window. I immediately started surveying the room. I located the entrance to the bathroom, the remote for the TV was on the bedside table, and to contact the nurse or other staff or to control the light switch you had to push the built-in button that was on the inside of the bed rail. I was sleeping so much that I lost track of days and time. There was a huge chalkboard in front of me. I am positive that all the names of the people that were caring for me are on the board. Today's date would be written on the board as well, but I couldn't see any of it without my glasses. "Where's Marcus? How are the kids? Who's taking care of my family?" These are the thoughts that were running through my head. I began to pray that God would continue to watch over my family and I. I was unable to finish my prayer because I fell fast asleep.

Suddenly, there was a knock at my door. Dr. Lydia Wang entered my room, pulled up a chair next to me and sat down.

"Hello, Mrs. Henson. You've had quite an ordeal. How is your pain right now?"

"Are you experiencing any tingling or numbness?"

Before I could answer any of her questions, she removed the covers on the bed to expose my legs. Next, she touched my right toe then moved along my right foot then up my leg. I couldn't feel her touch, but I could see the bandages and some type of drainage tube was hanging from my leg. There was no cast on my leg. She lifted my injured leg using both hands.

The pain was excruciating. This was the beginning of many sharp piercing pains that ripped through my leg.

Dr. Wang explained the surgery procedure and that the results were good. She spoke so fast I was barely able to keep up. She explained that the tibia and fibula bones in my leg were badly damaged in the accident. A permanent metal rod was inserted to provide strength and support the bones in my leg. The metal rod started at my knee and traveled all the way down to the ankle area. The rod was held in place by screws at both ends.

"How long is the healing process? When will I be able to walk again?" I asked.

"The process will take three to six months," Dr. Wang replied.

"SIX MONTHS!?!?!"

"Yes, ma'am six months" she repeated again. "Do you have any more questions for me?" she inquired. When I didn't have any questions, she proceeded to exit my room. Hopefully her next patient will receive better news than I did.

The surgeon who performed the surgery arrived in my room about an hour later. He announced himself as Dr. Lee. He discussed many of the same topics as Dr. Wang did. Dr. Lee also shared some bad news. I was scheduled for a second surgery in several hours. The drainage tube would be removed, and instead of a cast, I would be given a lightweight boot to wear for several months. The stitches would be removed at a later time. He left and once again I was alone with my thoughts.

Another surgery sadly meant no food for me, and I was getting very hungry. Right about now I could surely take pleasure in having a ribeye steak cooked well done topped with a couple of ounces of Heinz 57 steak sauce, some steak fries and a Caesar salad with a tall glass of sweet tea with lemon. However, that was not happening today!

A short time later, a team of staff members arrived. The phlebotomist drew more blood, the nursing assistant took my vitals, and a port-a-cath (IVAD) was installed in my chest. The device was placed under my skin as it would allow for me to receive medications and a blood draw. Then I was transported out and the second surgery was done. Everything went well. I was moved to recovery for a while then back into room 410 in just a few hours. I was still attached to a catheter which allowed my urine to flow into a bag. I also had a machine that recorded most of my vitals every fifteen minutes. The blood pressure cuff was still wrapped tightly around my arm. I was not in any pain, but I was still very sleepy from the anesthesia.

The smell of food filled my room. I thought that I was dreaming but I wasn't. There was a meal waiting for me on the bedside table. I was so hungry. I couldn't wait to lift the top that was covering the meal. I was afraid that the tray was delivered in error. I started eating that food so fast that I nearly choked. I wanted to finish the meal before someone decided to take the tray away. The thin slice of honey baked ham was awesome along with the green beans and the mashed potatoes. I ate everything on the plate.

Marcus finally came by the hospital to visit me. I was glad to be alert and awake to talk to him.

"Hello, it's good to finally see you," I greeted him.

"Hello, it's good to see you too! That was a really bad accident," he responded.

"I only remember bits and pieces of it. I remember being on the ground looking up trying to figure out what was going on," I replied.

He continued on, "Well a private emergency vehicle rear ended the car that rear ended you. The young gentleman that rear-ended you was very frightened but unharmed. He also had his 18-month-old brother riding in the back seat."

"WHAAAAAT!?!?" I exclaimed.

"Yes, Vera but Thank God he was properly secured in a car seat because the car was pushed into our neighbor's living room. Don't worry, the child was safe. As a matter of fact, when they finally got him out of the car he was laughing," he said.

"My Goodness!", I replied.

"Since you were standing behind the cars looking at the damage when the emergency vehicle hit, the force of the impact knocked you into the air with such a powerful momentum. Even though you landed in the street in seconds it knocked you under the emergency transport vehicle which is what you were seeing in your confusion." He said in a stern tone. I couldn't believe that I had survived this ordeal.

"How are the kids?", I asked.

“Simone is just fine but Melvin hasn’t eaten anything in two days.” This news was very depressing to me.

“I’ll call the kids. Maybe if they hear my voice and know that I will be home soon, they will be okay. What about my eyeglasses?”

“They were broken and unrepairable," he said.

“Well, do you have any good news?” I asked.

He laughed and replied, “My carpool friends and I are going to start working longer hours. That would give me the opportunity to make extra money. I have to go now but I am really glad to see you are ok.”

After Marcus left, I began to throw myself a pity party. Marcus didn’t even ask how I was doing. He didn’t give me a hug, and he forgot to give me a kiss. I started thinking about Melvin, poor Melvin. He witnessed the entire accident and now isn’t eating. The kids and I do not have any type of medical coverage, and the hospital stay is going to cost thousands of dollars. On the other hand, Marcus had full medical coverage with his job.

My leg was starting to hurt again and this time I knew that my pain level was at a ten. I hit the call button for a nurse to request pain medicine. Once it was administered, I drifted off to sleep.

The following day, the physical therapist came in to see me. His name was Jeremiah. He stood in front of me with a wide grin on his face and had a walker in his hand. Evidently, he didn't have all the facts because I had no intention of getting out of this bed to walk anywhere. The pain was still unbearable. "I cannot walk today. Not today", I told him. He simply said, "Ok, we will try again tomorrow", turned around and left the room.

My mother arrived the following day. I was really happy to see her. Things always went well with Mom on the scene. She had arrived home earlier from a bridal showcase in Plano, Texas. Lea's Bridal Salon was booming with business and that made Leona Williams very happy. She always said that her cup runneth over. Mom asked me to sit up in bed and I did just that. She whipped out a wide-tooth comb and a firm brush from her purse. She swiftly began to comb my hair out. Next, she parted my hair into two sections. The feel of her hands massaging my hair and scalp was therapeutic. She brushed my hair and then combed some more. The end result felt awesome. I had two beautiful braids - one on each side of my head. Not once did I think about any pain while she was working on my scalp and my hair.

There was a small mirror inside the bedside table. I pulled the table closer to me, took it out and took a closer look at my face. I could see some small scars on my forehead, but I was still here. Mom sat down next to me on the bed and softly spoke these words to me,

"Vera, we are all entitled to a pity party from time to time, but God has spared your life from a terrible accident. You are alive! Now it is time for you to get out of this bed and start living again."

My mother always spoke what was on her mind. She is a kind and affectionate woman. She hugged me so tight then she left. She had to fly back to Dallas in a few hours.

My bladder was full, and I needed to go to the restroom. My catheter was removed per the doctor's orders. I think that I am being forced to get out of this bed. My legs were swollen twice their normal size. I was afraid to walk. Anxiety had taken total control of my mind and my body. Just then the door to my room opened slightly. It was Jeremiah the physical therapist. He tapped on my door as he was opening it and was now standing in my room once again with the same walker he had with him yesterday. He took one look at my face and knew I wouldn't fight with him today. If I was ever going to walk again, I had to start today. Dr. Wang would be discharging me soon, and I couldn’t hide in this bed forever.

Jeremiah assisted me in sitting up on the side of my bed. Several minutes later, I was standing putting most of my weight on the left side of my body. He placed a gait belt around my waist to help prevent me from falling. The walker was placed in front of me. I grabbed each side with both hands. Jeremiah encouraged me to take a step. This was not easy at all. I moved the walker forward just a little bit. Then, I took a step with my left foot, and I slowly moved my right leg to where it would be standing right beside the left leg. I didn’t put any pressure on my right leg. I didn’t bend my injured leg either. Jeremiah was right by my side. We were going to make this happen today.

I moved the walker forward again, took another step with my left leg and swung my right leg over next to me. We repeated these steps several times. He assisted me in walking to the restroom that was only five feet away. I made it! The toilet had a raised seat on it with a safety rail. As I was sitting there, I started thinking about how you never know how much you appreciate your legs until you truly have a need for them one day. Jeremiah waited patiently for me as I finished in the restroom. It felt so good to wash my hands with hot soap and water. We finally made it from the restroom back to the bed. I apologized to him for my behavior the day before. He replied, "No problem at all. Healing gets better with time. We will walk again tomorrow."

I placed my call light on for the nurse. I needed something for pain. Those sharp pains were back again stronger than before. Between the pain I was in and the hospital staff in and out of my room all night, sleep and I couldn't connect to one another. I could hear the sound of unanswered call lights beeping all night long. I wished that Marcus had thought to bring my cell phone and a couple of more items. I welcomed my own toiletries such as Jergens lotion, a bar of Dove soap and deodorant. It's been a few days now and I need to take a real shower. The hospital's idea of a bath is giant disposable washcloths that feel like they have been put into a microwave oven.

Dr. Wang arrived early the next morning. My discharge date has been scheduled for tomorrow. She suggested that I produce a bowel movement prior to leaving the hospital. She made it sound so simple. Jeremiah was true to his word. He arrived early in the morning as well to do physical therapy. He assisted me in sitting up on the side of my bed like he did yesterday. Today, I was wearing two hospital gowns. I needed my front and back to be covered while walking.

Together, we walked outside of my room and all the way down the corridor. He reminded me to not put any pressure on my right leg. He didn't have to tell me twice. My energy was disappearing, but I had to hang on because this was the beginning of a long ride. We finally went back to my room. I scarcely made it to the restroom without any assistance from Jeremiah. Jeremiah was slowly smiling at my success. He didn't know that I was terrified and afraid on the inside. Tomorrow I would go home and there would be no one to take care of me. Now I know how my clients feel. They are all alone most of the time, and that's why my business was important. I love being a caregiver. I love the people I take care of. This is what I do, but now I need a caregiver too.

Ready or not, my discharge date has arrived. Today I am going home. Marcus arrived an hour ago with a tote bag. The tote bag contained a blue jean dress, undergarments, and one single shoe for my left foot. Marcus packed all of the items that the hospital gave to me in the same tote bag including the discharge instructions. Jeremiah stopped by my room and escorted me to the elevator. Marcus walked beside us carrying my walker and the tote bag.

While we were waiting for the elevator, there were at least a dozen young teenage girls also waiting to catch the elevator. They were beautifully dressed in white scrubs and pink sneakers. I knew who they were and what they represented the moment I saw them. The girls are here to volunteer their time and energy in assisting the hospital staff in caring for the patients. They are called candy stripers. The elevator finally arrives to the fourth floor. The doors were opening and there were more candy stripers aboard. They were very kind to make room for Marcus, Jeremiah and I. We made it to the first floor without any stops. Marcus' Chevy Tahoe was parked in the front of the hospital entrance with the hazard lights flashing.

Melvin got out of the front seat to greet me and offer support. I was so happy to see him and to know that he was okay. Jeremiah pushed the wheelchair very close to the Tahoe. I followed all of Jeremiah's instructions. I was standing facing Jeremiah and was attempting to enter the vehicle in a backwards position. I tried as hard as I could to get in, but the pain was unbearable. Jeremiah and Marcus had to lift me up and into the rear of the Tahoe. I used my good leg and foot to push myself all the way over to the other side so that both of my legs were stretched out on the back seat. I thanked Jeremiah several times for his assistance. He was a great caregiver and physical therapist.

As Marcus was driving home, I was thinking about the candy stripers in the hospital. I would have been a great candy striper. I made the phone calls almost every other week for two years. I was told that they would call me back when there was a position available. As a child, I believed that volunteers were always needed. On this day, I didn't see any volunteers that looked like me. There didn't appear to be any African American candy stripers, and that made me sad.

Marcus arrives home a few minutes later each night. He always opens and inspects the fridge in search of something to eat. Most of the time there are leftovers, but we have reached a period in our lives where everyone must take care of themselves. After eating, Marcus always takes a shower and later sneaks outside to have just a few more puffs on his cigarette. He has known for years that I have asthma and the smell of smoke is not good for my lungs. My symptoms are under control, and I have not visited the emergency room in quite some time. I can smell the strong stench of smoke in Marcus' freshly washed hair. When you love someone, you think that you can endure each and every thing. I am sure that this theory is no longer working for us.

The kids are home from school today due to the teachers having a meeting. They are excited because I have finally agreed to get out of the house. Melvin and Simone helped me walk out of the front door and down the front steps. I am really nervous, but I am putting on an excellent front. So far, things were going fairly well. We made it to Marcus' Tahoe in one piece. I was riding in the backseat with my healing leg stretched out. My other leg was on the floorboard firmly in place as if I had access to the brakes. It was time to start praying for a successful mini road trip. Melvin is driving and we are on our way to the Department of Motor Vehicles. If all goes well, Melvin will pass the test to obtain a driving learner's permit. He has all of the necessary documents, and he feels that he is ready. Melvin parks the car under the perfect shade tree.

I decided to relax and maybe take a small nap. Simone decided that this was a great opportunity to ask me a million questions. "Mom," she inquired, "Where are we going on vacation this summer? Is anyone going to teach me how to drive soon? When are you going to get a new car? Do you think that we can eat out today?" Simone fired off a series of questions. My responses were a mix of uncertainty: "I don't know; maybe; hopefully soon and maybe." The prospect of a nap slipped away. Suddenly, I spotted Melvin approaching the car, his expression inscrutable. Opting for silence, I decided to see how the cow ate the cabbage, as the old saying goes—telling the unvarnished truth, even if it's not what someone wants to hear.

Melvin entered the car without uttering a word. Starting the engine, he exited the DMV parking lot. Simone sat in the front seat beside Melvin, turning to make eye contact with me in the rear seat.

Lips parting, she whispered, "He failed the test!" Simone's lack of whispering skills was well-known. Melvin burst into loud laughter, elevating my blood pressure and startling me. "I passed the test!" he exclaimed, filling the car with uproarious laughter. Melvin's talent for humor and lightheartedness was evident, turning what seemed like a serious moment into a joyous occasion.

Melvin decided to take the scenic route all the way home. We drove past the Lorraine Bailey Motel which is now The National Civil Rights Museum. The ride brought back memories of walking down Beale Street and visiting the Peabody Hotel. I remember getting so excited about the Memphis in May Festivals. I wish that we could dine out and enjoy some good Bar-B-Que, but it would have to be another day. I told Melvin that it was time for us to go home. We needed to replace the gas in the Tahoe and get the vehicle safely back into the driveway. The last thing that I needed was for Marcus to come home and find the Tahoe missing in action. Marcus would surely go into a cardiac arrest.

Melvin made one last stop which was very close to home. He was pumping gas while Simone went next door to pick up dinner. It looks like we are having pizza for dinner again.

I managed to get out of the Tahoe with a little assistance. Simone had my walker waiting for me as soon as I made my exit. My body was so stiff that I could barely move around. With the help of the kids, I made it up the steps and into the house. The kids and I were seated in the dining area. We were laughing and joking around as usual and then the front door opened. Marcus had arrived home early from work. He washed his hands and joined us for pizza. It was just like old times. We were all sitting together and enjoying the food. Marcus stated that there was a power outage at the plant and all of the workers were sent home.

Later that night, I decided to take a real shower. I was so afraid that I would slip and fall. Marcus gently placed my booted leg inside of a large trash bag. He applied some gray plumbing tape around the top of the trash bag. This would prevent my boot and leg from getting wet per the doctor's order. This was truly a balancing act to make this happen. I have used this technique many times with several patients over the years. I am praying that the same technique will work for me. Our tub has glass shower doors which will not allow me the flexibility that I needed but I was determined to take a shower today! I am standing naked as a jaybird in a very small bathroom with Marcus.

I am able to finally get into the tub. The sensation of the water spraying the front of my body is glorifying. Marcus passes me a washcloth with some Dove body wash applied. I was able to wash most of my body, and it felt so good. Marcus used a different washcloth and began to wash my back and other areas that I could not reach. The towel rack and the handle on the shower door assisted me in maintaining my balance during the duration of my water shower. I used every drop of hot water that was available. The hot water tank was small enough to fit under the cabinet near the kitchen sink.

Marcus helped me get out of the shower. The small bathroom was now foggy, and I was afraid to move around. I did not want to fall and reinjure myself, and I certainly did not want to fall and cause harm to Marcus. I was so happy that he could read my mind. He left the room. By him doing that, it gave me the much-needed space needed to move around. I was exhausted long before bedtime. It was Friday night, and the kids would most likely stay up late. I was sitting on the edge of the bed wearing an old and unattractive red nylon nightgown. After removing the plastic bag and the remaining tape from my leg, I inspected the boot for water damage. The boot was a little damp, so I decided to sleep without the boot for one night. I removed the old bandages and cleaned my leg very well before applying new bandages. The procedure was done without any assistance. I was so proud of myself. I was actually making some progress. A short time later, Marcus was making an attempt to crawl into bed quietly. The sound of the squeaky wood flooring and the strong smell of nicotine from the Kool 100's cigarettes, forewarned me that he had arrived.

Our relationship had started to change throughout the years. We became more like roommates rather than the intimate connection of husband and wife. Marcus seemed to have achieved all his desires in life—a house, a truck, a wife, and two children. On the other hand, my aspirations revolved around establishing a caregiving business and exploring beautiful destinations with my family. I held onto the belief that if two people truly loved each other, they could find common ground. Regrettably, this has not happened for us, not yet.

The attorney handling my case has reached out to me on multiple occasions, consistently urging me to schedule an appointment with the recommended physical therapist. Seeking guidance, I phoned my Mom to get her opinion on the matter. I counted the rings waiting patiently for her to answer. When she finally picked up, I said,

"Hey Mom. How are you?"

"Hello, my dear" she replied.

"Well the attorney has been reaching out suggesting I go to physical therapy. What do you think?"

"Well Vera, maybe you should go to the therapist. They may be able to speed up your recovery process."

I gave her input a lot of thought. I had made some gains in my healing process, but I didn't think that it was fast enough. Given my ultimate aim of returning to my passion for caregiving, I decided to take action and called the attorney to arrange the initial appointment.

Three weeks later, with the grace of God, I am seated behind the wheel of the Tahoe. My handy walker was riding beside me in the front passenger seat. I could hear my heartbeat pounding loudly in my eardrums as I managed to drive the vehicle out of the driveway and onto the street. Driving with my left foot wasn't so frightful until I had to make a stop at the redlight. I applied enough pressure to the brake pedal that could have caused me and everything in the car to go flying through the windshield. I did not look around to see if anyone was watching. I had to pretend that I was the only driver on the street that day. I had an appointment with the physical therapist in one hour and I have plans to be there on time.

Upon arrival, I was greeted by a very tall young man. His name was Malik. After being seated and out of breath, I was given several documents to fill out and sign. Malik stated that he would be my PT for today's session. Malik spoke English with a distinguishing accent. I wanted to ask Malik what country he originated from, but I did not want to offend him in any way. I was instructed to change out of my clothes and into purple scrubs made of paper. All of my personal belongings were to be placed in a locker in the dressing room. There were eight lockers available, and each one held a key. Each locker was labeled with the name of a country such as Ghana, England, France, Greece, Ireland, Italy, Switzerland, and New Zealand. I would love the opportunity to visit at least one of the countries. At the present moment all of my belongings were placed in Ireland.

I followed Malik with my walker to a large room containing exercise equipment, giant balls, and lots of other gadgets that I was not familiar with. My journey was unique. Malik asked me to sit in a large chair that was facing a gigantic bowl like container. Later, he removed my right pant leg with a pair of scissors exposing the wounded area. He removed the boot from my leg and the bandages from the wound. Malik placed my leg inside of a container which was almost filled with fluid of some kind. The fluid level was deep enough to cover my leg from knee to toes. I was instructed to sit back and relax, and then he disappeared.

After a while, the temperature inside of the container was getting really hot. After a few more minutes, it felt like the skin was actually being boiled right off of my leg. This was definitely a BOILING POT! I began to panic, and started shouting loudly, "HELP!". Malik arrived just in time to remove my leg from the boiling pot. I started surveying every inch of my leg. The wounds were healing very well and there were only two noticeable marks. One scar is the size of a silver dollar, and the other blemish was much smaller in size. I would have these disfigurements for life, but I thank God every day that I survived. Malik towel dried my leg and applied a much smaller bandage than the larger bandages that were normally put on my leg. He also placed the walking boot on my leg. I am so looking forward to no longer needing the boot.

My next step was learning how to walk up and down three steps. The facility had a set of wooden steps that were very similar to the ones located near my front porch. I did not think that I could accomplish this goal, but Malik was firm, and I had to do it. He took the time to educate me on the correct way of going up and down the stairs when you have an injured leg. After his explanation, I realized that I did not use the correct alignment or distribute my weight properly when leaving the house today. I made it down the steps by the grace of God.

After therapy today, I retrieved all of my clothing from Ireland and got dressed in my blue floral print dress. I slowly walked to the Tahoe using my walker and drove away. I had convinced myself that my driving skills were up to par and decided to stop at McDonald's drive thru to treat myself to something good. I ordered a large piping hot french fry that tasted really good. I also enjoyed some sweet tea. I made it home safely and parked the Tahoe into the driveway. I truly had a very productive day. When the kids arrived home from school, they found me asleep on top of the bed. I was still holding the keys in my hand. "Did you go somewhere today?" Simone asked. "Yes, I went to Ireland," I replied.

Over the next two months, I made several more trips to physical therapy. It was very difficult to be present at all of my appointments. We only had one vehicle and it was only available during the weeks that Marcus was not the assigned driver of the carpool. My pain level has decreased, and I am walking faster every day. The wheelchair is no longer needed but I am keeping the walker until I have completely healed.

My attorney, Franklin H. Jones, requested that I come into the office. He is aware that I am not interested in going to court. My main objective was to make sure that all of the medical bills were paid in full. The paralegal explained all of the details regarding my case over the phone. She said that after the attorney fees, medical bills and other billable items were paid, I would receive a check for the remaining unused funds. Twenty-six days later, the kids and I made the trip to the attorney's office. Melvin found the perfect spot which was close to the front entrance. The kids asked to stay in the car. I got out of the car, walked the short distance to the attorney's office and took a seat. The attorney was expecting me and there were no other clients in the office. My signature was applied to several documents. I received a packet which contained the police report, several legal documents and a check made out to me. The amount of the check was less than my annual salary.

As always, Melvin opts for the scenic route on our way home. Simone bursts into laughter at something amusing on the radio, and I relish the view from the backseat. Contemplating the blessing of being alive and having healthy, happy children fills me with gratitude. Uncertain about the future for Marcus and me, I find solace in the belief that with God, all things are possible.

Chapter 4

Behavioral Health

The kids and I finally made home after a day at the park. I grew up in the park that we visited today. Pine Hill Park and I shared many summers together. The camp counselors were awesome. However, learning how to swim was one of my greatest oppositions because I was afraid of water. Eventually, I became a really good swimmer. I often wondered to myself if the kids were old enough to take swimming lessons. As I was entering the house, I noticed the light on the answering machine was blinking. I pressed the play button to play the messages. The first message was from a telemarketer. I didn't have a clue as to what he was selling. Now the second message was of great value. I had to hit the button again.

"Hi. This message is for Vera Henson. We have a position available for a patient care assistant in our behavioral health center. The hours are

Saturdays and Sundays, 16 hours each day but you can receive a rate pay of up to 40 hours a week due to shift differential for working on the weekends."

I thought to myself how awesome is this. The message continued,

"If you are interested, please call me. I'm Rebecca Reya and can be reached at 901-248-9632. I'll be looking forward to hearing from you."

I replayed the message a couple of times because I wanted to make sure that my ears were processing everything correctly. Marcus was going to have a stroke when he heard about this. He would not like the idea of me being away from the kids every weekend. On the one hand, I had already made up my mind that I was giving Ms. Rebecca Reya a call first thing in the morning. On the other hand, maybe I should talk to Marcus about the new position over dinner tonight.

We had leftovers for dinner. We had fried chicken - legs and wings - with mashed potatoes and gravy. I tossed a salad because we ate all the green beans yesterday. The kids stayed up a little later than normal. I gave Melvin and Simone their bath and put them to bed. I wanted them to be asleep when I made that important phone call in the morning. Marcus had to leave early that morning because it was his turn to drive in the carpool. I woke up the next morning and prepared myself for the phone call with Rebecca Reya. When the time came, I dialed the number she left on the voicemail.

“Good Morning, may I speak with Rebecca Reya please?

“This is Rebecca speaking.”

“Well hello there my name is Vera Henson. I received a voicemail from you yesterday about a position in patient care you had available.”

“Yes, thank you so much for returning my call.”

She went on to explain the position and its requirements. The conversation was going really well. Just before we got off the phone, I couldn’t help myself but to ask.

“Hey, I'm curious, how did you find out about me?”

“Oh, you know that ad you ran in the Sunday morning paper? It was brilliant! My staff and I have had a great laugh about you in our staff meetings.”

Now I knew that I had a good sense of humor, but maybe the joke would be funny to me at a later date. Ms. Reya quoted my salary, and I was very happy with that. I was promoted from a private duty sitter to a patient care assistant in a mental health facility.

I couldn't believe all of the good news I was hearing. The kids and I would finally have health insurance. I would finally get paid vacation, and a 401k. What could go wrong? I was still eager to learn, but I wasn't quite sure if I was prepared for mental health. Ms. Reya asked me to come by the facility to take a tour and fill out all the necessary paperwork the following day. My instructions were to go directly to HR on the second floor.

When I arrived, there was a ton of paperwork for me to fill out. Each form had a lot of questions. I completed a drug screening that included a urine specimen. I was fingerprinted, and my photo was taken for my ID badge. I was told by a clerk in HR that I would need to take a CPR course within six months because my card would expire in 180 days. I didn't have any experience in behavioral health, and I was very happy that this position provided on the job training. The clerk in HR escorted me to the sixth floor where I would be working. My ID badge was the credentials I needed to enter the elevator to the sixth floor.

I met with Ms. Reya and a few of her staff members. The sixth floor looked deserted to me. I later found out that most of the patients were out on a field trip to an AA meeting. The remaining patients were attending a relaxation class. The staff didn't wear standard uniforms. They wore regular attire. I can only assume that the patients didn't have ID badges otherwise there wouldn't be a way to tell the patients from the staff.

After leaving the facility, I went to my Mom's house to pick up the kids. I wanted to get home in time to fix Marcus' favorite meal, and during dinner I had planned to deliver the news about the new job. The spaghetti and meatballs were ready in no time at all. I made a fresh salad adding onions, bacon and two boiled eggs. The smell of the garlic bread was a favorite for the whole family. I broke the news to Marcus as he took his last bite of food. The house became really quiet. All of a sudden Marcus said, "I think you are biting off more than you can chew." I didn't reply. Marcus was quiet for the remainder of the day. He never said another word.

I reported to work the following Saturday morning at 6:45 AM. Everyone at home was still asleep, including Marcus when I left the house. Four hours into my shift, I was ready to quit and run home. While working at the nurse's station, a beautiful young lady with a beautiful head of hair and a great smile, walked over to me and asked for a pair of scissors. I opened up a couple of drawers until I found a pair of scissors and I handed them to her. She said thank you and walked down the hall to the third door on the right side of the corridor. This was her room I assumed.

After continuing to read a note at the nurse's station and some of the other reading material that Ms. Reya had put aside for me to review, I would have never been prepared for what happened next. The same beautiful young lady that asked for the pair of scissors was once again at the nurse's station. She was returning the scissors. She had taken the scissors and cut off all of her hair except for three strands. She was bald headed! I was frozen. I couldn't move or take a step. I could barely breathe because I couldn't believe what was happening.

The patient's name was Gina. She was admitted to the sixth floor about three weeks ago for an eating disorder. Gina was a twenty-seven-year-old white female weighing in at about 92 pounds. The staff immediately jumped into action. She was taken to her room and placed on suicide watch for the next twenty-four hours. An incident report was written by the head nurse and the doctor was notified. I also had to fill out a portion of the incident report. I had to explain how and why I gave a patient a pair of scissors. After all, I was the culprit.

Suicide watch at the behavioral health center was a workout. I had the pleasure of making rounds and observing Gina every fifteen minutes for the remainder of my sixteen hour shift. This was not a punishment. It was part of my job description. David, one of the mental health technicians on the floor, gave me a break several times throughout the night. He was my relief. David appeared to have a good personality. He worked well with the staff, but he was very firm with the patients.

He shared with me several important facts about patient care on the sixth floor. The number one rule: No sharps. I looked at David and he repeated it and went on to explain himself. David said, "No sharps, no scissors, no razors, fingernail files, fingernail clippers, shoestrings and no outside drugs of any kind." David went on to explain that sometimes patients may become suicidal and may use sharp objects to harm themselves. I thanked David for the tips. It had been a rough day. When my second shift ended at 11:00 PM, I drove straight home, checked on the kids, jumped in the shower and twenty minutes later, I actually fell in the bed with Marcus and went fast asleep.

It's Sunday morning around 6:00 AM and everybody is still asleep. Before I left to go to work that morning, I decided to set the table for my family. The table was beautifully set for a party of three. I got out a box of Kellogg's Corn Flakes and a box of Cheerios. The bowls and everything else were already on the table. All Marcus would have to do is provide the milk. I hate that I was going to miss church services today, but most of all I was going to miss spending time with the children. I had to look on the bright side. I had all week to spoil Melvin and Simone.

The second day on the job was a whole lot better than the first. We had eighteen patients on the floor. Gina was still on suicide watch. Today was family day. The patients had the opportunity to spend quality time with a family member. We had a family room where the patients could spend time with their families. All visitors had to leave all items in a container at the nurse's station. They could not take their coats, handbags, or any other outside items into the family room. The reason for this is because sometimes family members would bring in unacceptable items into the unit. Sometimes they bring items that they think that the patient should have. Today, I had the opportunity to assist with checking in family members.

The first step is a staff member must go down to the first floor and escort all visitors to the sixth floor. The visitors have to sign in and check their belongings. After being checked, they were allowed to go into the family room. Sunday was a great day. It was quiet and there were no AA meetings. It was good. Two weeks later, I had the pleasure of attending an AA meeting. AA is for Alcoholics Anonymous. These meetings were held outside of the facility. David would go down to get the van and bring it around to the front of the facility, while another nurse and I would escort the patients down to the van. The AA meetings were sometimes at different locations, but today this particular meeting was about twenty minutes from the facility.

It gave the patients an opportunity to get off the floor and get out to see some different surroundings. We had to be very watchful with the patients and watch them every minute. After the meeting was over, David and I took the patients to Walgreens so they could pick up personal items such as toothpaste, deodorant, and lotion. The females most likely would be purchasing sanitary products.

One of the patients, Tina, decided to steal some laxatives from Walgreens. Now Tina has an eating disorder. I can't remember if she was bulimic or anorexic, but if she was in our program she suffered from one of the disorders. We didn't realize that she had stolen the laxative until several hours later. I am pretty sure that she used the entire package of laxative. Tina spent the remainder of that shift throwing up and experiencing diarrhea. I was assigned to watch Tina for the remainder of my shift. That was worse than the suicide watch because every time that I went to check on Tina, she had accidentally pooped everywhere. All over the toilet, all over the bathroom floor, and if she wasn't pooping, she was throwing up. Guess who gets to clean that up? Me.

Tina had a special order from the doctor. She was required to eat. Her meals were high-calorie meals. Tina had it in her mind that she was overweight. She considered herself to be fat when in actuality she weighed a whopping 100 pounds soaking wet. I had to observe Tina a week later while she was eating her meal. I guess I wasn't paying close attention as there were eighteen patients eating in the same room. Tina would take the little margarine containers that were 100 calories each and rub it on her legs and thighs along with her arms so that she wouldn't consume the 100 calories of margarine.

Now I didn't notice this right away. It was a good day, and everyone was enjoying their meals. I didn't catch it but after lunch when everyone went about their way, the head nurse called me into the office. He said, "Vera, I want you to take a look at this video." I said, "Sure not a problem." It was me in the video. I could see where Tina was applying the margarine to her legs, thighs, and arms. The head nurse, Steven, asked me to follow him to Tina's room immediately after eating her meal. Tina was confronted about the eating incident, and she was informed that the doctor would be notified. Steven made notes in the patient's file and the incident would be discussed in tomorrow's staff meeting.

As I have said before, I am glad that there was on-the-job training. I ended up staying at the behavioral health center for three more years. I watched patients go in and out. I sat through many staff meetings and learned more about those patients than I wanted to. At the end of those four years, I had to rethink some things. In those four years, I didn't get a chance to attend Sunday Services maybe once or twice a year or maybe on vacation. It's been three years that I spent away from the children. They were now older, so I needed to do family time with all four of us together.

The only good thing that I could say is that I got a lot of experience with behavioral health. It really opened my eyes to take notice of people. People that look just like you and me. They have a lot of problems going on in their lives and you're not able to tell because we are looking at them from the outside. The other good thing is that I was able to save quite a bit of money in my 401k and I know that I will be able to do some good things for my children to make their lives better.

Chapter 5

Contracting with Agencies

Marcus and I had been walking on eggshells for some time now. I was working almost every weekend for four years and wasn't aware of the strain it was putting on my marriage. Maybe, he needed a break also. I started working for an agency contracting to do home aide visits. The job description consisted of assisting clients with bathing, changing the bed, and light household duties, preparing light meals, and grocery shopping. It also consisted of keeping notes of the clients, vitals and all the services that we provided to them. All visits must be completed within one and a half hours. If the time needed to be extended, we would have to contact the agency to get permission. The agency paid a flat rate of $20.00 per visit. I knew that this would be good for me because of the flexible hours.

My first patient was Mrs. Mary Hayys. According to the case manager and the nurse, Mrs. Hayys was an eighty-six-year-old single African American woman. She was non ambulatory (meaning that she was not able to walk), 5'6", and 124 pounds. Mrs. Hayys is wheelchair bound, lives alone, has no children, and her only emergency contact is her brother Ralph Hayys. Mrs. Hayys was set up for visits seven days a week, twice daily - one in the morning and one in the evening. I was scheduled to provide home health visits for Mrs. Hayys from Monday through Thursday. All of the visits were scheduled for the mornings. Mrs. Hayys lived in the Walnut Grove area of Memphis in a really nice condo on the first floor.

I appeared at Mrs. Hayys' door around 9:00 AM after using her gate code to enter into the gated community. The door was unlocked. I entered and immediately started calling out her name as soon as I crossed the threshold. The condo was spacious with hardwood flooring. The furniture was antiquated but well kept. I could hear Mrs. Hayys shouting, "Here I am" in a crisp low tone voice. I made my way to her bedroom listening to her voice. "Lord have mercy!", I cried out. I was instantly placed into panic mode. Mrs. Hayys was hanging from the ceiling in her bedroom upside down. There was some kind of homemade contraption that was drilled into the ceiling. It had the pattern of railroad tracks going around in a circle. There were also three or four chains hanging from the ceiling which were attached to Mrs. Hayys. The chains were attached to a wide belt that was around her waist. It was operated by a handheld remote. Mrs. Hayys had dropped the remote on the floor.

"Good Morning Mrs. Hayys. My name is Vera Henson, your new home health aide. How can I help?"

"Could you please pick up the remote off the floor and hand it to me?" she replied very calmly.

I picked up the remote and I placed it up into her hands. Mrs. Hayys began to push the buttons on the remote. She pushed the button on the contraption as it was swinging her body forward and backward in a jerking type motion. The end result was she was supposed to land in the wheelchair which was located at the end of her bed. However, this was not happening today. Mrs. Hayys was now dizzy and a little weak from hanging upside down. I raised her hospital bed up as high as it could go. Between the both of us, we were able to get the remote to operate and land her safely onto the bed with my assistance. I took Mrs. Hayys' vitals; her blood pressure was a little high. Her care plan stated that she should have a shower. She had her own shower chair. Her bathroom was specifically designed to push the wheelchair into the shower to give herself a shower, but today I would be giving her a bed bath. This would allow her to relax and lower her blood pressure. I found the necessary items needed to complete her bath.

After her bath, I dressed her in clean clothes, and I lifted her onto the wheelchair. I pushed her wheelchair into the bathroom so that she could brush her teeth, comb her hair, and apply her makeup. Mrs. Hayys had excellent upper body strength. Everything else from the waist down had very little movement. She requested that I fix her a cup of black coffee and wanted two pieces of raisin bread to be toasted with some orange marmalade spread from the refrigerator. I prepared the coffee and toast, and then took her vitals again. Her vitals were much better. I made the bed and made sure that the bedroom and the bathroom were cleaned. Approximately ninety minutes later, Mrs. Hayys signed my paperwork from the agency, and I was on my way.

Another home health aide would arrive later in the day to put Mrs. Hayys back to bed. When I got to my car, I called the agency to report everything that had happened during my morning visit with Mrs. Hayys.

I had the pleasure of working with Mrs. Hayys for five years. She was a very friendly lady, and I always enjoyed my visits, but I was always prepared for a surprise. The following year, my daughter Simone wanted to travel with me to work. This was a school project, and it was only for one day. What could go wrong? Simone and I arrived at Mrs. Hayys' home around 9:45 AM sharp. It was against company policy for anyone other than a staff member or someone being trained to see any of the patients taking a bath at any time or without any clothes on ever. I had already received permission from Mrs. Hayys to bring Simone with me to work that morning. She was excited to see Simone.

The agency knew absolutely nothing about the take your daughter to work project. I helped Mrs. Hayys with her shower and helped her get dressed. Mrs. Hayys had a really good grade of hair and after shampooing her hair, I noticed that she was a really pretty lady. I began to realize that she wanted to wear the same hairstyle - just a little ponytail. I left Mrs. Hayys alone so she could apply her makeup while I went to check on Simone. As soon as I turned the corner Simone replied, “Hi Mommy. Don’t I look pretty?” Mrs. Hayys always kept a large roll of postage stamps on a small table near the sofa. Simone had taken the postage stamps and made a necklace, two bracelets, and ten fake fingernails out of the postage stamps.

I was able to snatch off all of the jewelry and the fake nails before Mrs. Hayys rolled her wheelchair into the kitchen. Today Mrs. Hayys requested croissants with the orange marmalade spread. While Mrs. Hayys was enjoying her breakfast, I motioned for Simone to go with me and observe as I put clean linen on the bed and tidied up everything. I placed all of the dirty items in the washing machine and pressed the start button after adding Tide detergent. The PM aide will put the clothes in the dryer when she arrives. I told Mrs. Hayys that I would see her in the morning. Not a word was mentioned about the postage stamps.

Simone and I had lunch at Burger King. Burger King had a special today - two complete meals for $7.00 plus tax. We blessed the food, and I spoke to Simone about the postage stamp situation. I explained to her that we should never take things that don't belong to us. We ate our lunch, and I talked some more. We stopped at the post office and picked up a large roll of stamps. A large roll of postage stamps costs more than my wages for today. Mrs. Hayys was my only patient for today. I decided on that day that I would be contracting with other agencies soon so that I could always have a full schedule.

Later that day, I told Marcus about everything that happened at work. Marcus was laughing so hard as if I was telling a joke. I said, "Ok. Ok.... next year Simone will go to work with you. I am going to start looking for a hardhat and some steel toe boots in her size." Marcus laughed even louder. The following day, I switched out the postage stamps. Now Mrs. Hayys would have a full roll. I don't think that she'll ever notice that the stamps were missing.

I signed up with agency number two as a home health aide. Agency number two offered a rate of $20.00 per visit, offered reimbursement for mileage as well as bonuses. This was awesome. Agency number two called and asked if I would make a visit to Mr. Kevin Stovall. Mr. Stovall lived near the intersection of Winchester and Shelby Drive. Mr. Stovall was a seventy-seven-year-old widow who was injured in an automobile accident two years ago. According to the agency, Mr. Stovall is able to walk with some assistance, has a housekeeper, and his emergency contact was his son Jerry who visits often to take care of him. His son keeps the refrigerator stocked with lots of fruits and precooked meals.

Mr. Stovall could take care of a lot of his personal needs, but he would not shower unless someone was standing right outside of the shower because he was very afraid of falling. Mr. Stovall completed his shower, and I assisted him with putting on clean clothes. He chose a medium gray two-piece jogging outfit for this day, and he even allowed me to shave his face. This was my first time in a long time shaving a man's face, but I didn't tell Mr. Stovall that.

The visit only lasted about thirty minutes. I asked Mr. Stovall if there was anything else that I could do for him before I left. He developed a strange look in his face and his eyes were huge. I didn't know what to think. I did not know what he needed. Mr. Stovall asked me to push his wheelchair close to the garage door. He opened the door and asked me to take a look. I locked his wheelchair and stood on the two stairs leading to the garage so that I could peek. There were two antique cars, and they were beautiful.

Mr. Stovall asked if I would turn the ignition on in the car and let the car run for a while. I didn't see anything wrong with that as it was a small request. He gave me the keys that he retrieved from a rack in the kitchen, and I cranked the car up. I got out of the car and walked around it - a beautiful lime green antique car. I walked back up the stairs and I asked Mr. Stovall what type of car it was. He proudly announced that it was a 1969 GTO Judge Convertible. I had never seen anything like it.

About a minute later, Mr. Stovall asked me to go back into the garage and rev the motor. "Ok. What is this all about?", I asked myself. So I pressed the accelerator and revved the motor. "I just wanted to listen to the sound of the engine," he said. The sound of the engine really excited him, but the smoke and the smell from the exhaust was not only in the garage but it was now entering the living area into his home.

We both began to cough uncontrollably, but he did not want me to cut off the ignition. I thought to myself, "Ok Vera. How are you going to get out of this mess?" All of a sudden, the front door opened and in walked my Mr. Stovall's son, Jerry. Jerry walked past his dad and I, walked down the steps leading into the garage, and he turned the key. The car was no longer running. Jerry raised the garage door and walked back up the steps, closing the door, and began to open several windows in the home. He did all of this without saying a word. Jerry was over six feet tall. His dad and I were both looking up to him. I was waiting for a screaming match to start. I was glued to my one spot and frozen in time as well as speechless. Jerry walked over to his dad and said, "It looks like you are having another bad day dad."

Mr. Stovall just sat in his chair and looked like a little child with his hands caught in the cookie jar. I, on the other hand, opened my mouth to speak and not one word would escape through my lips. So I just closed my mouth. The younger Stovall signed my paperwork, and asked if I would do more visits with his dad. I simply nodded yes and speedily left. I never visited the Stovall's again. I was just filling in because Mr. Stovall's regular home health aide was out sick, and I wondered why.

I really enjoyed doing home health throughout the years. It requires a special talent from God and a lot of love for the people that you take care of. Caregiving is one of my greatest accomplishments besides being a wife and a mother to two beautiful children.

I got a call from the agency to do a PM visit to Mrs. Mary Hayys. It happened on a very hot summer day. I arrived at her home at around 4:00 PM and no one was home. I called the agency. The agency said that the nurse had arrived there at 2:00 PM and that Mrs. Hayys was there. I started wondering to myself where in the world could Mrs. Hayys be. She could not walk, and her neighbors were upstairs, and I am sure that she didn't go to visit them. All of a sudden, I heard this strange voice say to me, *"Go to the swimming pool."* Now I know that I had been driving around all day. Maybe I had spent too much time in the hot sun. I heard that voice again, *"Go to the swimming pool."*

So I walked over to the swimming pool and saw her wheelchair and one of her ruby red towels initialed *H.* Mrs. Hayys was in the swimming pool very close to the edge of the pool. She was not swimming but was holding on to the edge for dear life. Javier, the gardener, arrived a few seconds after me. Javier and I were able to lift Mrs. Hayys up out of the pool and safely onto her wheelchair. I took her ruby red towel and wrapped it around her. Javier didn't speak much English, but together we were able to get Mrs. Hayys across the rough pavement and back to her condo. Javier left.

I placed a light blanket on the top of her bed. I took off her swimwear and gave her a bed bath. As I was applying lotion to her skin, I examined her for sunburn and any tears on her skin. I checked her vitals, and her blood pressure was good. Her pulse was good, and she did not have a temperature. I removed the blanket and positioned her in bed. She was not hungry, but I left a fresh banana nut muffin and a vanilla Ensure at her bedside table for her to eat or drink later. There were clothes in the washer, and I moved them to the dryer and turned the dryer on. The agency received a call from me a little after 5:00 PM to report the pool incident. The conversation ended with a question,

"Who put the swimwear on Mrs. Hayys in the first place?

"It was the gardener," replied Mrs. Hayys.

She went on to tell me that it cost her $20.00 to have some fun in the swimming pool. Priceless!

Chapter 6

Lady's Best Friend

I arrived at the home of Mrs. Bowman on a late Friday afternoon. Mrs. Bowman will be my last client for today. Today has been a tough day for me. My allergies had been acting up all day. There were twelve steps to climb, before I was able to make contact with the doorbell. I could hear multiple dogs barking in the background as soon as I pressed the doorbell. The agencies that I do contract work with all know that there are a million reasons why I don't work with dogs. The main reason that I don't work well with dogs is because I have asthma and I am allergic to dogs and cats, not to mention that I have a huge fear of getting bitten. Besides that, dogs don't like me. They can smell my fear from miles away.

I could hear the frail voice of an elderly female asking,

"Who is it?"

"Vera Henson from the agency," I replied.

"I am your home health aide for today."

I am pretty sure she could not hear one word that I said due to the harmony of the barking dogs. There was no time for me to run away. Mrs. Bowman was now standing at the wooden front door. There was another door made of glass and that allowed me to get a quick view of what I would be walking into. It took Mrs. Bowman forever to get the glass door unlocked. She was working so hard with her arthritic hands to open the door. I was not in any hurry. There were two humongous Great Danes, who were barking louder than bass drums, greeting me at the door.

Mrs. Bowman finally got the door unlocked. She was much shorter than I am and about half of my size. I was so afraid to enter her home, but I did. I begin to pray because I think that my day has just gotten rougher. The small mansion was a wreck. There was dog poop and dog hair everywhere as far as I could see from the entrance hallway. Mrs. Bowman has seven oversized Great Danes living in her home. The home smelled of stale cigarettes, lots of smoke and only God knows what else. For me, this was a recipe for disaster. I knew that I would not last long in this atmosphere. My throat and lungs had started to swell. I had to convince my legs to start walking and trailing behind Mrs. Bowman and her family of dogs. They were her family and I had to respect that.

Mrs. Bowman stated that she was looking forward to taking a good bath. I was thanking the Lord that this was a home health aide visit and not a private duty sitter assignment. Mrs. Bowman looked really tired and a lot older than seventy-one years old. The dogs continued to bark, and all eyes were on me. All of the dogs were grayish in color, and they all weighed over one hundred and forty pounds. I increased my steps so that I could march right beside Mrs. Bowman. That was impossible because she held a leash which was attached to one of the dogs. His name was Bo.

Bo rested on my foot most of the way to the bathroom. The bathroom door was locked. Mrs. Bowman's wrist held a key bracelet which was securing the key to the locked bathroom door. Once the door was open, I knew right away why she kept the door locked. I think that the bathroom was the only clean room in her home. The bathroom was immaculate.

Mrs. Bowman's bathroom looked like something out of a home improvement magazine. The room was around two hundred square feet. It contained a huge garden tub and also a walk-in shower, a savannah chaise lounge that was surrounded by beautiful pictures of island scenery. This was not just any old bathroom, but it was also a room where someone could go to escape.

I asked Mrs. Bowman if she would allow the dogs to go outside while she was taking a bath. She did not like the request, but I had to insist, not just for her safety, but also for my safety. Mrs. Bowman was upset, but I would not bend. "I will not put Bo outside. The other babies are okay to go outside but not Bo. Bo is blind and is in bad health", replied Mrs. Bowman.

Mrs. Bowman reached out her hand and gave me the leash that was attached to Bo, then she proceeded to the patio door to let the dogs outside. I hung my jacket and caregiver bag on the back of the bathroom door after I retrieved a mask and a pair of gloves. I also managed to get two quick puffs from my inhaler. I began to fill the tub with water and added the body wash that Mrs. Bowman had resting on the side of the tub. Bo was sitting very quietly. He was not paying any attention to me and that was just fine. When Mrs. Bowman returned to the bathroom, she was no longer angry.

I assisted her in removing her clothing and getting into the tub. Mrs. Bowman enjoyed getting her back scrubbed and she had a full conversation with Bo the entire time that she was in the tub. I washed and put conditioner on her hair. I do not think that she has washed her hair in some time, but that's okay. Her hair was getting a great wash today. After bathing, Mrs. Bowman got dressed in a royal blue robe and placed a navy-blue bonnet on her head made of terry cloth. She looked like a totally different woman.

It was time to clean the bathroom. As Mrs. Bowman was leaving the room, I reminded her that Bo wanted to go with her. I did not want to take a chance of falling on Bo, considering Bo was resting on my foot while we were in the bathroom.

As I was tidying up, I began to wonder if taking care of so many dogs has taken a toll on Mrs. Bowman. The dogs are larger than her, and it must cost a fortune to feed and take care of them. The dogs have destroyed her home. I know that they are a part of her family, and I have to respect her decision to take care of her fur babies.

I am hoping that Adult Protective Services will never show up at her home. Her living conditions are unhealthy and deplorable. She would most likely be removed from her home and the dogs would end up at the shelter. I will have to report the situation to the agency. Hopefully they will make the best decision for all parties involved. My allergies are starting to get out of control, and I needed to take Benadryl and try to make it home before the medication put me to sleep.

Mrs. Bowman was making her way toward the patio door. The bathroom was clean. I gathered all of my belongings and headed for the front door. As Mrs. Bowman was sliding the glass patio door open, I began to say goodbye. I could hear the barking and the family would soon be hot on my trail. I made it out of the front door just in time. I had doggy poop on my shoes and lots of hair on my uniform.

The cool air felt really good blowing against my face. I took two more puffs from my emergency inhaler. I was not feeling my best and I needed to get out of this uniform to change into some fresh clothes. Maybe I could make a stop at the nearby McDonald's and change my clothes there. I searched through the trunk of my car to see what was available. I found an old red flannel top and matching red pants inside of a bag that I had every intention of dropping off at the Goodwill. I do not like wearing this outfit because the kids say that I look like Santa Claus, and I totally disagree. I also found a pair of flip flops that I keep in the car to use whenever I get a pedicure.

I made it to McDonald's and was able to change my clothes in the restroom. I peeled off my clothes very carefully and stuffed everything inside of my uniform pants. I could not allow any more dog hair to come in contact with my body. After I had accomplished my mission, I ran and jumped into the car. I did not want anyone to see me in this Santa outfit. It took me a few minutes to catch my breath. I started the car and drove through McDonald's drive thru and placed an order for a large sweet tea. I rushed to take the Benadryl and wanted to make it home before I fell asleep behind the wheel.

When I pulled into the driveway a very short time later, it appeared that no one was home. I remained in my car just a little while longer, so I decided to take a quick nap. Pretty soon, all of the troubles of today just simply faded away. I rested over the weekend and made every attempt to enjoy time with my family. Once again, I was a survivor. There wasn't any need for a trip to the emergency room because I was able to give myself a breathing treatment at home. I love my family and I did not want them to worry about me. I loved being a caregiver.

The following Tuesday, I received a phone call and a text message from the agency. Mrs. Bowman called the agency very early on Monday morning. She expressed to the agency that she would love for me to be her permanent home health aide. I did not have any problem informing the agency that this was a request that I could not honor. I am unsure how the agency handled the situation, but I am sure that Vera Henson will not be visiting Mrs. Bowman's residence anytime soon.

Chapter 7

A Good Laugh

I was sitting in my car reading a flier that someone had placed on the right window blade. The flier advertised that the fair would be arriving in Memphis in two weeks. Melvin, Simone, and I always enjoyed the festivities. Marcus rarely attends any family functions because he is very conservative when it comes to spending money although one of us would have to remember to bring home a smoked turkey leg for him.

I placed the flier on the rear seat and got out of the car to visit Mrs. Lyza Moore. Mrs. Moore is a cheerful, sixty-something year old female that is so polite. She developed some type of high cholesterol disease which resulted in both legs and thighs being amputated. The agency never provides sufficient information regarding a patient's health. Being a home health aide has taught me to ask any questions necessary in order for me to provide the best care. Mrs. Moore's door is always unlocked when I arrive. She is able to see me as I walk up the sidewalk towards her door. She has a significant other who is rarely in town. I have worked with Mrs. Moore for four plus years and have only seen Clarence four times.

After taking her vitals, I assisted Mrs. Moore with a tub bath today. We have a unique system that works very well. I fill the tub nearly half full of water with lots of bubbles. Mrs. Moore wheels her chair over, parks right next to the bathtub, and locks the wheels. I stand in front of her and the wheelchair, and then lean forward so she can lock her hands around me. Next, I placed my hands firmly on her hips. On the count of three, I lift her with a little swing and down into the tub. Mrs. Moore usually takes it from there. She can bathe herself and shampoo her hair.

She enjoys the times that I come to visit her. While she is taking a bath, I am usually changing the linen on her bed or sometimes I just need to make the bed. Whatever is needed is what I do.

I assist Mrs. Moore in getting out of the tub with the same steps used to put into the bathtub. After her bath, Mrs. Moore is able to transfer herself from the wheelchair to a comfortable lean back chair in the living area. Mrs. Moore has a dog named Tilley.

Tilley is a light brown cocker spaniel who spends most of her time outdoors. Sometimes when I visit, my allergies would flare up. I am allergic to dogs, cats, and many species of plants and trees. Rapidly, Tilley runs into the living room from the doggy door. Tilley has a live bird inside her mouth. Mrs. Moore starts yelling at Tilley to take the bird back outside. Tilley opens her mouth to bark at Mrs. Moore.

The bird was no longer being held a prisoner in her mouth. The bird started making noise as it was flying around the room. Our visit now seems to have turned into a circus. I didn't sign up for any of these activities. I ran as fast as I could into Mrs. Moore's bedroom. I could hear Mrs. Moore, Tilley and the bird continually making noise. I also heard Mrs. Moore laughing her heart out and asked me to join them in the living room. She laughed and she laughed, and she laughed.

The bedroom window would not open for me. I thought this would be my chance to escape. Mrs. Moore did not have a back door. I stayed in the bedroom for about fifteen minutes or so. I walked down the short hallway and into the living area when the atmosphere was quiet. Tilley and the bird were nowhere to be seen so I pretended as though nothing happened. I told Mrs. Moore that I would see her again. She signed my paperwork, and I left the building. There was still no sign of Tilley and the bird. When I got to my car, I thought to myself, "What a day...what a day." I will make another visit to Mrs. Moore.

Wintertime in Memphis can be very brutal. Today's temperature is a balmy forty-four degrees, and it will dip into the low twenties tonight. Mrs. Moore is my first client on this crisp, cold Wednesday morning. When I arrived at her home, near Airways and Ketchum, I noticed that her gold wingback chair was sitting outside close to the curb. The chair was flawless, and I was wondering why in the world was her best chair sitting at the curb. How did it get here? I entered the home as always and saw Mrs. Moore in the living room sitting in her wheelchair. She was not her usual cheerful and talkative self today. Something was definitely amiss. Without the chair in its usual place, the living area appears much larger.

I got out my blood pressure monitor and other tools to assist in taking her vitals:

B/P 120/70

Pulse 78

Respiration 18

Temperature 97.8 degrees Fahrenheit

Mrs. Moore's vitals are good. She didn't want a bath today. Her bed was already made. I asked her, "What can I do for you today?" She didn't give a response to the question and continued to give a solemn look on her face.

A short time later, Mrs. Moore was sitting in the front passenger seat of my car. She was wrapped up like a Christmas snowman, or should I say *snowlady*. I made sure that her seatbelt was secured. Mrs. Moore didn't have legs and I didn't want her to fly should anything happen while I was driving. We were on our way to Royal's Furniture Company on Lamar Avenue. It was so cold outside. There were only a few drivers out today. We arrived at the furniture store. I helped Mrs. Moore out of the car and into her wheelchair. Once inside the store, she selected a beautiful pale yellow reclining chair.

She asked the salesman if the chair could be delivered today. He promised her that the chair would arrive at her home within two to four hours. She was excited to hear that and then retrieved her credit card from the inside of her ruby red hat she wore on her head. She purchased the chair, and the salesman gave her a sales slip along with her credit card. Mrs. Moore placed the items back in her hat. We returned to the car. After assisting her with the seat belt, I placed her lightweight wheelchair into the rear of my car.

On the ride back, I asked Mrs. Moore, "Are you ready to tell me what happened to your chair?" She looked at me and said, "You have to promise me that you will not laugh when I tell you." I nodded in agreement, and she went on to explain that she has arachnophobia. I knew all about arachnophobia as both of my children are deathly afraid of spiders. Mrs. Moore continued on to say that she fell asleep in the gold wingback chair. She was awakened by something crawling across her right shoulder. She slapped her shoulder with her left hand and killed a spider. She became very frightened and yelled out for help very loudly.

Her neighbor next door ran over to check on her. Mrs. Moore told the neighbor about the spider and her fear of them. She asked him to remove the chair from the home. I didn't laugh and didn't think that the situation was funny. All of what she explained to me I understood. During her explanation, we arrived back at her home, and I helped her get back inside from the cold air. I hung her coat in the closet and fixed her hot chocolate in her favorite coffee mug. Her home was warm and inviting. The new chair was due to arrive soon.

After the visit, I walked back to my car and noticed that the gold chair disappeared. I wondered who came and got the chair. I also wondered that if they knew there was possibly a nest of spiders in the chair would they have still taken the chair. No one will ever know the answer to that question. We are all afraid of something or someone. Sometimes, life presents us with many different phobias whether big or small. My list of phobias continues to grow from year to year. Fear is never funny.

Chapter 8

The Great Escape

The holidays are approaching swiftly, and I have not completed my Christmas shopping list. It's early November and the Christmas catalogs have already started to consume most of the space in our aging mailbox. Marcus and I briefly discussed working extra hours so that the holiday spending would not disturb our fixed household budget. I decided to work a few hours with Karegiver Relief Services. Their office is located on the other side of town, but they had several clients that lived within a twenty-mile radius of my home.

The staff appeared to be very friendly, and they were happy to hire employees with experience. My first assignment was an eight-hour shift from 3:00 PM until 11:00 PM on Friday. My caregiver bag was packed and ready to go.

I double checked to make sure that I had my water bottles, some snacks, phone charger, hand sanitizer, a flashlight, notepads, and a few personal items.

I arrived at the home of Ms. Jazzy Ketchup around 2:30 PM. Karegiver Relief Services provides around the clock care for Ms. Ketchup. Per the agency, Ms. Ketchup is a seventy-year-old female who is in fairly good shape, a little over four feet tall and weighs around 98 pounds. Ms. Ketchup has early-stage Alzheimer's and we must keep a close eye on her at all times. Arriving early has always been a great pointer for me. This usually allows me the opportunity to talk to the present caregiver or family members to gain more insight about the client that I will be working with.

That did not happen today. As soon as I knocked on the door, the caregiver that I was relieving bolted out of the front door so fast that she nearly knocked me down.

"Hello, I'm Essie. Sorry, I have to rush out. Please read the notes in the red notebook, which is on the kitchen table. Ms. Ketchup is looking forward to seeing you. Bye" said Essie.

At 2:45 PM, Essie was driving her chocolate Camero down Shady Grove Road. I entered the home of Ms. Jazzy

Ketchup, moving slowly through her home and calling her name with every three steps. I did not receive a response. At the moment, it feels like something was crawling on the back of my neck. I am in a security guard mode as I am checking each and every room in the small, two-bedroom home in search of Jazzy Ketchup.

My search ended with a small prayer.

"Lord, I need you to help me to locate this missing person", I prayed.

As I was praying in the bathroom, the shower drapes punched me in my lower back. I could not move to save my own life. I stood frozen until I heard someone crying behind the shower drapes. I slowly turned around and moved the drapes all the way over to my right side. Ms. Ketchup was standing in the shower wearing pink pajamas stating that she was lost and would like to go home. I helped her out of the shower. She was no longer crying.

“You’re at home. You’re safe at home.” I explained to her.

“My name is Vera Henson. I’m your home health aide and I’m here to assist you. What’s your name?” I asked her.

"Jazzy,” she replied.

This is how my shift started! I took Jazzy by the hand and escorted her into the kitchen. Jazzy immediately selected the chair at the head of the table. I assumed that this was her permanent place at the table. After taking a quick inventory of the fridge, I quickly became aware that someone who lives at this residence loves ice cream. I prepared Jazzy a small bowl of french vanilla ice cream. While Jazzy was indulging the cold treat, I quickly reviewed the care plan and also made eye contact with the notations in the red notebook. It appears that Ms. Jazzy Ketchup will only respond to being addressed as Jazzy.

Jazzy has no diet restrictions, a good appetite, and is incontinent 50% of the time. Jazzy does not have any children and only one living relative, her nephew and emergency contact person Robert Ketchup. Jazzy was once a famous hairdresser for the rich and famous. There were plenty of notes that mentioned early-stage Alzheimer's and to make sure that all doors and windows are locked at all times. The notes also provided the four-digit code to the security alarm. I made a mental note to keep the security alarm armed at all times.

Around 5:00 PM, Jazzy was working on a puzzle, which she seemed to really enjoy. At 6:00 PM, dinner was served. Jazzy devoured two medium sized salmon croquette patties on a bed of rice and a small salad. I offered her a glass of water and about one half of a can of Dr. Pepper. She gave me many compliments on how good the food tasted. Jazzy was unaware that the fridge was stocked with plenty of pre-cooked and ready to heat and serve meals as well as fresh fruits and a ton of ice cream. Jazzy was taking a bubble bath when the phone started ringing at 8:00 PM. I hurried to answer the phone. The agency was calling to inform me that the relief person for the following shift had canceled due to a family emergency. They asked if I would be willing to work a double shift. I agreed to work the double shift this time.

When you are a caregiver, there are times when it may be necessary to work longer hours than anticipated. I have learned that especially during the holiday seasons, unexpected things may happen. Being prepared has always been successful for me. It's 10:00 PM and Jazzy is wide awake, snacking on some green seedless grapes and watching some pre-recorded showings of *Dancing with the Stars.*

She looks like a miniature version of Barbie. Jazzy is wearing a set of hot pink pajamas with matching house shoes. As a matter of fact, I think that all of her sleeping garments are pink. I am working on a load of laundry and tidying up a few things around the house. I gather that Jazzy is resting her eyes. According to the notes. Jazzy rarely sleeps and never sleeps in her bed. She likes to take small naps in the recliner while watching television. I am going to allow her to achieve that goal while I take a bathroom break. Maybe I will have a few more minutes to eat my peanut butter and jelly sandwich that I also packed in my bag.

Around midnight, Jazzy and I started working on some arts and crafts. She was wide awake with a ton of energy. I was happy because she was happy. I asked her several times throughout the night if she needed to go to the bathroom. She was a willing participant every time. We did not have any incontinence issues that night. It's almost 2:00 AM and Jazzy is listening to music with her headphones on. She likes all types of music, and she will sit and listen to her music for hours. Sometimes, I think she is asleep and then all of a sudden, you can hear her humming or clapping her hands. I can imagine that Jazzy was an amazing woman before she started to develop memory loss.

Jazzy was finally asleep in her recliner. I was getting sleepy and hungry myself, but the thought of taking a nap was not possible. Plus, I would never eat any of my client's food. I placed a blanket over her so that she would stay warm and maybe stay asleep for a couple of hours. I did some writing in the notebook. I wanted to be sure to leave good notes so that the next caregiver would have up to date information. I made my rounds throughout the house to make sure that all of the doors and windows were locked. Jazzy loves to open doors and windows according to the notes left by previous caregivers.

The table was set for breakfast and the clock has started to move at a snail's pace. Jazzy is awake and crying. She had gotten out of the recliner, and now the both of us are occupying the same space. She is requesting to put on her boots. It's almost 6:00 AM on Saturday morning, and we are searching for a pair of boots. I located a pair of clear rain boots and from the expression on Jazzy's face, these are not the correct boots. There was a shoebox on the very top shelf inside of Jazzy's closet. I am tall, but the shelf was taller than me. I walked into the hallway and borrowed an umbrella from the coat rack. I used the umbrella to assist me in retrieving the shoebox, which was long enough to reach the pair of boots. After opening the box, Jazzy immediately put the pink boots on and danced her way out into the hallway. I think that we have located the correct boots. I left the shoebox at the foot of the bed and returned the umbrella back to its original place.

It's now 7:00 AM, and I have been awake for twenty-four hours. The house phone is ringing, and at the present moment, I am only welcoming good news. I answered the phone in my corporate America voice. "Hello, this is the Ketchup's residence," I said. The call was from the agency. The female representative from Karegiver's Relief Services was very apologetic and her speech was awesome. I only remembered a few words from the phone conversation, HELP IS ON THE WAY!

This Saturday morning, Jazzy was having french toast for breakfast. I still had a few Ritz crackers and a Butterfinger from my caregiver's bag, but my energy was fading. My body was moving in slow motion, but I was still hanging in there with Jazzy. I wanted to get the kitchen cleaned and have everything looking good before the relief person arrived. Jazzy is in the bathroom brushing her teeth. She loves to comb and style her own hair. I assisted Jazzy in putting on Depends, which are adult incontinence underwear. Jazzy is also wearing a pink floral robe, pink pajamas and pink boots.

After tidying up the bathroom, I wanted to take out the trash. Jazzy insisted on walking with me to the outdoor trash can. I remembered to turn the security alarm off before we exited the side patio door. It was a chilly November morning in Memphis as Jazzy and I walked the short distance to the outdoor trash. Jazzy wanted to sit outside under the gazebo which was really beautiful. We did not stay outdoors for long because I did not have a clear view of the patio door and I was getting cold.

A short time later, Jazzy and I both were back inside where it was nice and warm. I locked the patio door and placed the security bar in place. Jazzy was once again in the recliner, listening to music with her headphones on. It's almost 10:00 AM, and I decided to sit quietly in one of the kitchen chairs after placing the chair near the door that the caregivers used for entering and leaving the home. Jazzy was asleep. I had all of my belongings together and was ready to roll out as soon as my relief arrived. I was so sleepy and closed my eyes for just a few minutes not realizing that I drifted off to sleep.

I didn't hear the car pull into the driveway or the closing of a car door. I was awakened by loud voices and someone knocking on the door. I took a quick look and Jazzy was nowhere in sight with the headphones sitting in the recliner. I moved the chair back into the kitchen. I ran throughout the house searching for Jazzy and she was gone. I did not have the time to have a panic attack because someone was now pounding on the door, and all I could hear was laughter. I unlocked the door and the relief caregiver walked in. She was carrying a large pizza box and a large bag from Macy's department store in one hand while hugging Jazzy with her other hand. "Hi, I'm Mary. Guess who I found walking down Shady Grove Road?", Mary replied. I was speechless. Mary was full of laughter and Jazzy was laughing too. I wanted to cry.

It was 10:20 AM and Mary was explaining to me that Jazzy had escaped through the doggy door. I told Mary that was impossible because I was sitting in a chair blocking the door. Mary continued to explain that Jazzy is a great escape artist. Jazzy crawled through the open space at the bottom of the chair and pushed herself out of the small pet door and went for a walk. I couldn't believe that she did that. Mary and I still talk and have made contact over the years. Neither one of us has ever reported the incident and as far as I know, the agency doesn't know anything.

Chapter 9

No More Cookies

Today, Ms. Tina Mae Brooks is celebrating her ninety-first birthday. She is ambulatory and can move faster than a superhero when she grabs a firm hold of her walker. Ms. Brooks is legally blind and loves to bake cakes and cookies. The agency assigned me to her more than two years ago. As her primary caregiver, I am responsible for assisting with her bathing needs, light household duties, meal preps, laundry care and grocery shopping. Ms. Brooks receives home health aide visits twice a day, five days per week as she is legally blind.

She lives in an upscale senior living community. Her entire apartment is approximately 2000 square feet. The fortress is large enough to entertain all of her twelve children and thirty-one grandchildren. She hasn't been able to keep an accurate count of her great-grandchildren. She is always happy to hear the grand news of a new addition to the family as they arrive.

After her shower, she selected a pale lavender pant suit with an off-white blouse to wear for her birthday celebration. The dining room is beautifully set and there are a few birthday decorations on the table and the walls. Ms. Brooks and I put up the decorations earlier in the week. In many of the conversations she shared with me, there were so many interesting facts about the family, and some were private. She faithfully loved all of her children. Ms. Brooks shared with me how she and her husband provided funding to put all of the children through college. They also provided for homes, fancy cars, and ventures. I have often wondered how does anyone obtain so much money. The guests should be arriving soon, and I have one more client to visit before returning later for her PM visit.

I double checked the carpet and other flooring before I left. Frequently, Ms. Brooks would have an occasional accident that would spill on the floor. She refuses to wear any type of incontinence products. I am praying that the birthday celebration will be heartwarming. Last year's celebration did not go well at all. Ms. Brooks was hospitalized for six days due to food poisoning. The diarrhea and vomiting lead to dehydration. This condition is not good for anyone, especially an older adult in their nineties.

I had to get going and complete a few assignments before returning for the PM visit. After completing the various assignments, I made a stop at Kentucky Fried Chicken. I wanted to make sure that my family had something for dinner. There was no way that I would be able to cook and do the PM visit at the same time. There were only two cars in front of me in the drive-thru. The family really enjoyed it when I stopped at one of the local restaurants to have dinner with them.

In preparation for dinner, Simone would usually set the table with whatever paper products we had available. We always had a variety of products to choose from because I purchased paper plates and cups, napkins, and other plasticware. I always managed to catch the items on sale after New Year's, Valentine's Day, Easter, and any other holidays. A 90% off sale is a bargain that I refuse to miss.

The food from KFC was satisfactory and the family size bucket was just perfect for all of us. Tonight, no one will have to wash dishes and Melvin will take the trash out. During dinner, Melvin discussed his upcoming football game. Simone mentioned that she needed several poster boards for another school project. As they were talking, Marcus left the table to go outside. He is not aware that I noticed he started smoking again. I enjoyed dinner with the family, but I was being very watchful of the time. Ms. Brooks will be expecting me soon. Sometimes I feel like I am always running towards something, but when I get there, I have to run some more!

As I was driving my car in reverse to get out of the driveway, Marcus waved goodbye to me. He could only hold the smoke for so long before exhaling to release the smoke from his lungs. When I returned to see Ms. Brooks for the PM home health visit, I stood on the outside of her door to listen before knocking. It was quiet for a party that should have started already. I knocked on the door and no one answered. I turned the doorknob to open the door as I have many times over the last two years. Ms. Brooks didn't answer when I called out her name loudly. I walked throughout her home, and I finally saw her sitting near the piano with both feet on her oversized ottoman. She was asleep.

There were two new beautiful floral arrangements on top of the piano along with a few birthday cards. I made several attempts to wake her up. She is usually a light sleeper. I took her vitals to make sure that everything was ok, and her vitals were good. I decided to get very close to her ear so she could hear my voice clearly. That seemed to work out quite well. She responded, "Oh hi Vera." When I leaned in to whisper in her ear, I figured out why she was not able to hear me right away. I could smell the liquor on her breath. I asked her, "How was the celebration?" as she was showing signs of returning to this world. She was not 100%, but at least we were now communicating.

Ms. Brooks stated that three of the children stopped by to see her; the oldest daughter brought her grandbaby with her to visit as well. She said that she had an awesome time and that she bonded with the baby very well. She also said that she had a glass of wine. I believed that she had one large glass of wine. Ms. Brooks struggled to get herself to a standing position. Between the walker and I, we made it into the master bedroom. I managed to get her out of her day clothes and into a nightgown. She refused to give me her dentures and mumbled something about being the birthday girl. I asked her if she would like to wash her face with the cleansing cloths that she normally uses every night and she replied, “No.” No was her answer for every question that I asked her this particular evening. I assisted Ms. Brooks with getting into the bed for the evening. She was sound asleep before I left to go home.

The next day I went for my normal AM visit. The smell of oatmeal raisin cookies was dancing in the air as I entered her home. There was flour everywhere. I saw at least four cookie sheets cooling on a rack. The racks could hold several dozens of cookies. Ms. Brooks has baked many cookies for me over the years and I have never tasted any of them.

She had already selected the garments she wanted to wear after her shower and requested that I put a rinse on her hair. I thought about this for a few moments before responding to her question. I have applied a rinse as well as color to my own hair many times, but I haven’t done this procedure for anyone else. I am not a beautician by any means at all. I finally agreed to put the rinse on her hair. I always have large disposable gloves with me at all times. The agency mostly supplies small or medium sized gloves for the home health aides.

In the bathroom, I was working nervously to get things ready for her shower and hair coloring. Ms. Brooks handed me a small gray plastic bottle. She said that she already mixed the contents together and the only thing that needed to be done was to apply the mixture to her unshampooed hair. Once completed, I would cover her hair with a plastic cap and leave it on for twenty-five minutes. I asked her, “Where were the instructions for this product?” I didn’t want to put any chemicals in her hair that would cause any harm to her scalp whatsoever. I now have a million butterflies in my stomach thanks to Ms. Brooks.

She is in the bathroom sitting on a small bar stool type chair facing the mirror. I put on my gloves and am applying the mixture to her hair. She is able to see my every move and has a happy expression on her face. Once the plastic cap was placed on her head, Ms. Brooks made a beeline to the shower. She was in the shower for more than twenty-five minutes. I used this time to start cleaning the kitchen area. It took forever to remove the flour from the floor and countertops.

I went back into the bathroom to check on Ms. Brooks. She completed a bowel movement and was attempting to clean herself. From the looks of her fingernails, it looks like she was having a tough time as usual. Sometimes she forgets to wash her hands, and that makes it difficult for me to keep her nails clean. I assisted her onto the shower chair with a different pair of rubber gloves on my hands. The water was warm just the way she likes it. I removed the plastic cap from her head. The butterflies in my stomach are now multiplied ten times over. Ms. Brooks' hair was now the color of a pink Easter egg. After washing and conditioning her hair, the color was still a powerful shade of pink that astounded me.

The hair coloring procedure has been completed. I wrapped a towel around the hair until I could locate the bag of rollers. She also had a shower and I paid special attention to her nails. Ms. Brooks is standing in front of the mirror with this huge smile while admiring her hair, which is now a shade of Easter egg pink. She was so happy, but I am currently terrified. How am I going to explain this to the agency and still have a job? I rolled up her hair using twenty-four medium sized rollers. She walked into the kitchen using her walker.

I began to clean the bathroom, picking up the soiled items and got the washer started. After everything was cleaned, I was ready to leave. I was happy that I didn't have to do the PM visit on this day for her. Today was overwhelming and I couldn't handle any more stress today.

Ms. Brooks placed several of her oatmeal raisin cookies in a Ziplock bag for me. She is one of the kindest women that I have known, but I will not eat the cookies. I usually put the cookies in the trash because I would never hurt her feelings. As I was walking to my car, I waved goodbye to Ms. Brooks. I placed the cookies on the floorboard in the rear of the car. At this moment, I needed to get far away from the pink hair, and I certainly did not want to see anymore cookies.

A few days later, the agency scheduled an in-office meeting for all of the home health aides. We often have monthly meetings to introduce new techniques or discuss changes in policy and procedures. Today's meeting was nice. The agency provided drinks, mini sub sandwiches and cookies courtesy of Subway. The meeting was very informative. I enjoyed the food. It was great to meet and greet with the other home health aides, nurses as well as those who work behind the scenes to make the agency successful. Just as the meeting was coming to a close, the scheduling coordinator, Pearl, asked,

"Does anyone know who decided to be a personal beautician for Ms. Brooks and dyed her hair pink?"

Everyone roared into a fit of laughter except for me. I didn't say anything at all even though I was the guilty party. I chose to use that moment to make a grand escape down the hall to pick up some supplies. I made it to my car without having to chat with anyone.

I decided to pick up the kids from school. Melvin got out of class earlier than Simone. Simone was always late getting to the car. She had to talk and laugh with many of her classmates before she would exit the school building. As soon as she got into the car, she started nibbling on Ms. Brooks' oatmeal raisin cookies.

Chapter 10

It's Getting Hot In Here

The agency called yesterday to ask if I would add Mrs. Jones to my list of home health aide visits for the day. I told them that I would give them a call back shortly. She lives fairly close to me, but decided to give her a call first to see if everything was ok. While speaking with Mrs. Jones over the phone, I had to use my concert voice because she was very hard of hearing. I told her that I would be there around 8:30 AM.

Mrs. Jones is not only hard of hearing, but she also speaks in a low childlike voice. I could barely hear her voice over the phone. I figured that the best way to start your day is with a client who lives near you so you can map out a route creating a circle. This will save you a lot of time and money as well as the wear and tear on your car. So I called the agency back and informed them that I wouldn't mind adding her to my visits for the day.

I parked my car on the side of the road, looked around and saw several cows, goats, and a dozen of mobile homes along with acres of land. I was officially lost. This happens often, and I have never gotten accustomed to it. According to my mapscope, I had arrived. All of a sudden, I heard someone call my name with a high pitch. It was funny because even the cows were disturbed by what they heard. "Vera, Vera.....over here!" An elderly woman was shouting from the last mobile home at the end. I waved my hand up high and shouted, "I'll be right there!" I felt a sense of security as I realized that I was no longer lost.

I got back into my car and drove down to a spot with very little grass. It was slightly hilly with a lot of small rocks, but much safer than parking on the side of the road. The lady was very short and friendly. She met with me outside as I introduced myself. I told her my name and stated that I was from the agency and would be Mrs. Jones' home health aide for the day. I knew right away that she knew all about me because the agency is known for informing the clients about who they are sending prior to the aide's arrival. The clients will know your full name, the type of vehicle that you'll be driving and a general description of what you look like.

Unfortunately, the agency is very limited with the information that they provide about the clients, especially the most important part, the care plan. “Please call me Odessa,” said the elderly woman. Ms. Odessa said that Mrs. Jones lives in the mobile unit that was facing her and that they have been friends for seven years. “Come on in. Mrs. Jones has been waiting to get a good bath for several days now” she said.

As I was processing the no bath for several days, a giant orange ball rolled slowly over to where Ms. Odessa and I were standing. I saw three small children running and laughing as they raced to retrieve the orange ball. The tallest of the children arrived first and said hello. We replied with a hello also. The children left to continue their game with the ball.

I followed Ms. Odessa into the home of Mrs. Jones, and she introduced me to Mrs. Jones. We all chatted briefly as I was getting settled. I lifted her care plan from the unique, oblong coffee table in the living area. The care plan stated that Mrs. Jones is a ninety-year-old female who is hard of hearing, weighs 140 pounds, and requires a tub bath. No vitals are needed. As I looked around, I noticed that her home was clean and very neat with no pets. All of the items needed for the bath were laid out on her bed; one blue long sleeve dress, one matching jacket, a pair of white mid-calf socks, underwear and one bladder pad along with a clear shower cap. Ms. Odessa went into the bathroom to semi-fill the tub with water. I watched as she added Suave body wash and a little Dawn dishwashing liquid to the water. Training is always appreciated whenever you enter a new client's home for the first time. Next, I saw Ms. Odessa attempt to light a gas wall heater to warm the bathroom to prevent Mrs. Jones from catching a chill. After four attempts of striking a match to start the wall heater, there was heat. I could never make myself perform this procedure because I am afraid of fire.

I went back into the living area to assist Mrs. Jones to the bathroom for her bath. She was able to stand with a little assistance. Ms. Odessa had the walker ready to go and Mrs. Jones placed her hands firmly on the walker, taking very small steps to achieve her goal of getting to the bathroom. I asked Mrs. Jones if she needed to use the toilet before getting into the tub. She didn't hear me. I got very close to her right ear and asked again. Mrs. Jones whispered in a small voice, "No." I asked her to sit on the toilet so I could undress her for the bath, and she did.

While Mrs. Jones was sitting on the toilet, I slowly began to undress her. I took off the shoes and then her socks. She assisted me in lifting the dress over her head. The fabric in the dress was so heavy; so I assumed that she was a cold natured woman who enjoys heat. I could hear urine falling into the toilet. The sound lasted a long time. Her bladder was now completely empty. With gloved hands, I assisted in applying several sheets of toilet paper to dry her.

Ms. Odessa had placed all of the dirty garments in the washing machine as I was putting on a new pair of gloves. I helped Mrs. Jones get from the toilet to the bathtub. Slowly, we pivoted and moved to the shower chair that was in the bathtub. It was really warm in the bathroom. I placed the clear shower cap over her hair. Ms. Odessa had provided all of the items needed to make everything a success. There were plenty of towels, body lotion, deodorant, and other items. While Mrs. Jones was enjoying the warm water on her feet, I knelt down on my knees, applied body wash to a washcloth and began to wash her legs.

Suddenly my heart was pounding in my throat. I developed a shortness of breath. There was a peninsula of sunshine circling the base of the bathtub on three sides. I could see the giant orange ball just beneath us. My ears could hear the children just underneath us. I started running the numbers in my head. Mrs. Jones' weight along with my weight was close to 380 pounds. How much did the bathtub weigh? Who will fall through the floor first? Lord, who will pick up my children from school? This is bad. It was getting really hot in here!

Ms. Odessa yelled from the living room, "Do you need any help?" I replied, "No, we are good!" Honestly, I didn't think that the floor could take the stress of additional weight. I started working with a little more speed! I rubbed soap over Mrs. Jones' entire body while watching the orange ball. I pulled the plug to let the water out and rinsed her very well. I dried her off in less than ten minutes and applied lotion to her entire body within seven minutes. I covered her with a large towel, went quickly into her bedroom and grabbed her change of clothes for the day. I almost forgot the deodorant. In twenty minutes, Mrs. Ruthie B. Jones was dressed and seated in her favorite lift chair in the living room.

I went back into the bathroom to clean the tub and to also make sure that everything was cleaned as it was when I arrived. I scooped up all of the dirty towels and other items to place them in the dirty clothes hamper. Thank You Lord for keeping me on solid ground. Ms. Odessa signed my paperwork, and I was on my way.

Chapter 11

The Six Dwarfs

The sun in Memphis has reached its highest peak. Between my hot flashes and the heat, I feel like surrendering and calling it a day. My cell phone is ringing while also receiving a text. I answered the phone, and it was the agency. They called to find out if I could do another visit. I agreed to the additional assignment. This visit would be outside of my circled area I created this morning. Mr. Rodney Hannah lived about twelve miles from the next red light. I was thirsty, hot and tired but I had to do my best in providing quality service. The agency provided a name, address, and phone number. This was not enough information for me to fill the space on a 3x5 sticky note.

I arrived at Mr. Rodney Hannah's home after climbing thirty steep steps up the stairs in the sun. The destination - apartment B. When I finally made it to the top of the stairs, there were six short men outside of Mr. Hannah's door. Three of them were standing and the other three were sitting on the concrete walkway. I asked them, "Is this the home of Rodney Hannah?" They all replied, "Yes." One of the men said that it was okay for me to enter the apartment. I opened the door and entered the small apartment. There was very little furniture, but the place was clean, and the air conditioning was cooling very well.

As soon as I took the seventh step into unit B, all hell broke loose. All the men who were outside were now inside standing right behind me. They were all trying to talk at the same time. I heard the front door being slammed closed, foot movement and a lot of other noises. One of them shouted, "I'm going first." A different voice said, "No. You went first the last time." The argument between them seemed to go on for days. I started to pray to My Father in Heaven. I thought that I was going to be raped and beaten to death. There was not enough strength in my body to fight off all six of them whether they were short or tall. Fear consumed my entire body, and I could not move. I couldn't turn around to bring myself to look at my attackers in their faces.

I forced myself to do the electric slide in slow motion to make my way towards the bedroom. I could see a picture of a room containing a hospital bed and someone was laying in that bed. I repeated to myself over and over again, "God, I am here to take care of Your people". In a sudden flash, all six men rushed past me into Mr. Hannah's bedroom. The men were carrying towels, clean sheets, and other much needed supplies into the bedroom. Finally, I was able to get into the bedroom to introduce myself to Mr. Hannah and the rest of the men in the room.

These men were very short in stature as well as very intimidating. They all had tattoos that covered most of their body parts, long beards, earrings, and lots of jewelry. I thought that they were members of a motorcycle club or something. They were not there to attack me. They were old army buddies of Mr. Hannah.

Many years ago, the army buddies made a commitment to each other. They vowed to take care of each other until the end of time. After they explained this to me, a sense of security fell over me and I began to calm down. I began to take Mr. Hannah's vitals. After completing that, everyone assisted me in giving him a shave and bed bath. Together we did oral care and changed the sheets on the bed. I have never experienced so much love in one room. This was so awesome. The gentlemen cleaned and put everything back in its correct place. Mr. Hannah signed my paperwork, and I was on my way.

As I was driving along the highway, I thanked the Lord for His Protection not only today but daily. From here on out, I am making a commitment:

To be a better caregiver

To offer a little more compassion

To be a better listener

To focus more on the needs of others

And....

To show more love whenever I can!

Chapter 12

It's Time For A Vacation

The rain has finally stopped and there are puddles and pools of water everywhere. The radio is playing one of my favorite songs by Bill Withers, *"Lovely Day."* Sometimes music can assist you in setting the tone for the day. Whoever said that music is good for the soul must have an awesome story to tell. I have finally gotten the courage to get out of the car and make a run for it before it decides to rain again. I am picking up a to-go order for Ms. Ross at a nearby cafe. I am definitely sure that the boxed lunch contains a Rueben the Great sandwich. Ms. Ross loves corned beef with sauerkraut with Swiss cheese and anything else that is available to put on her sandwich.

I arrived at Ms. Ross' home shortly thereafter. Her home sits on a corner lot and has several bay windows. You can stand at the corner and actually see Ms.

Ross moving around throughout her home because the wooden blinds are wide open at every window. She can see me getting out of my car and walking in her direction with the boxed lunch in my possession. Ms. Ross is eighty-something years old, hard of hearing and sharp as a needle. She is in fairly good health for her age and only requires a little assistance. As her home health aide my duties are to assist her in setting up her medications for the next seven days, change the linen on her bed every week, assist with laundry care and pick up lunch or a few groceries from the nearby Kroger's grocery store.

The nurse also comes out to visit Ms. Ross at least once a week. The agency provides home health services for Ms. Ross because she is an aging adult who lives alone and rarely leaves her home. She has one adopted son, who is a pilot and is rarely ever in town. They look forward to seeing each other whenever time permits.

Ms. Ross has two unique hobbies. She loves to create and design greeting cards and she is a professional sweepstake winner. Nothing surprises me about Ms. Ross. She takes great pleasure in showing me all of the prizes that she has won over the years. She was the grand prize winner of the home that she now resides in. She has lived in her prized home for the past thirty years. I am always excited to hear about her new winnings. Last month, Ms. Ross won a fifty-inch Sony television and a Visa gift card valued at five hundred dollars. I am wondering what in the world she will win next!

While Ms. Ross is enjoying her lunch, I will put fresh sheets on her bed and soon check the fridge to see which items will need to be added to the grocery list. I will also dispose of any expired items in the fridge. I always try to take just a few minutes at each visit to sit down and chat with most of my clients. Ms. Ross just happens to be one of my favorite people to work with. She is so full of life, and makes you feel welcome every time I enter her home.

I shared with Ms. Ross that I was ready for a vacation, and I wanted to go somewhere that I had never visited before. "Vera, I have just the sweepstakes for you," said Ms. Ross. She has tried many times to persuade me to enter several contests and sweepstakes. I did not believe that I would become a winner. As a matter of fact, she was the only winner that I knew personally, and I am excited whenever she wins. As I was getting ready to leave, Ms. Ross was putting together a small envelope for me.

The envelope contained all of the directions and items needed to possibly win a cruise to Mexico. We ended the visit with lots of laughter. "You can't win, if you don't try," said Ms. Ross. I promised her that I would enter the sweepstakes.

Later that night after putting away the clean dishes, I reviewed all of the items in the envelope that was given to me by Ms. Ross. I read all of the information and rules concerning the sweepstakes very carefully. Three winners would win a cruise to Mexico with all expenses paid, including roundtrip airfare for two people. This sounded too good to be true. Per the instructions, I had to write my full name, address, telephone number, and e-mail address on a 4x6 postcard and mail the postcard to a certain post office box. All of the entries had to be handwritten and postmarked no later than three weeks from tomorrow. There was a limit of ten entries. The envelope provided five postcards. Tomorrow, I will make a stop at the post office to mail out the five sweepstake entries and I will purchase a few more postcards. After all, a promise is a promise.

I made several more visits to Ms. Ross' home, and I always stopped by the cafe to pick up her Rueben the Great sandwich that she truly enjoys. Maybe one day, she will surprise me and try the Club sandwich. That's my favorite.

Several weeks later while working on a private duty case with a suicidal patient, I received a text. The text stated that I was one of three winners for the cruise to Mexico. I responded with a text saying YES, I would accept the trip. I did not have time to get excited because I had to stay focused while working. I could not allow anything bad to happen on my watch.

I received another text from my friend Karen. She informed me that my full name is being displayed on television in big bold letters as one of the winners of the sweepstakes. I responded to her text with multiple questions. I wanted to know who was the sponsor of the contest? Karen replied, "I don't know, but it has something to do with the TV show, *In the Heat of the Night*." Now I was excited.

Exactly two weeks later, I received the official documents in the mail notifying me that I was an official winner of a cruise, and the certificate to travel was good for one year. On my next visit to see Ms. Ross, I could not wait to share the awesome news. Ms. Ross called me a few hours prior to my visit to tell me that I did not need to stop and pick up lunch. Now this was strange, but nothing surprises me about Ms. Ross. When I arrived later that afternoon, I had to park my car down the street. Of course, the windows were open as usual, but I could see that Ms. Ross had some company. I got out of the car and walked over to Ms. Ross' place. The door opened.

As soon as I stepped onto the patio, there was a middle-aged man welcoming me with a smile. "Vera, come on in and meet my son Robert Ross," said Ms. Ross. As I was entering, I could smell pizza. The table was set and ready to serve. Ms. Ross insisted that I should join them for lunch. There was lasagna, shrimp pasta, pepperoni pizza with salad and breadsticks, from The Olive Garden.

"Please, call me Bob," stated Mr. Ross. I smiled, and replied okay as I was making my way over to the kitchen sink to wash my hands. The three of us sat and talked for some time. The meal was delicious, but it felt like they were having some type of private celebration. I did not dare ask! I was sitting there, all giddy inside, because I wanted to share my good news about winning the cruise to Mexico.

For some reason or another, I did not feel that the timing was right. Ms. Ross finally let the cat out of the bag. She stated that she has a new win, and it's a biggy! Once again, I am getting excited for her. “Mother has just won a brand-new, top of the line Chrysler minivan", said Bob. I was right, this is definitely a celebration. There was only one problem. Ms. Ross is not able to drive a car and most certainly, not a minivan.

"Vera, don't you have something to celebrate also?”, asked Ms. Ross. The woman is sharp as a needle. She knew that I was one of the winners in the sweepstakes. I should have known that she would stay on top of things. After all, she was the individual that made me promise to enter the sweepstakes. It was a very enjoyable afternoon. I assumed that Bob saw the look on my face when he made the announcement about Ms. Ross winning the minivan. He assured me that he and Ms. Ross had already taken care of the details.

According to Bob, this is not the first time that Ms. Ross has won a vehicle. Ms. Ross is going to sell the minivan back to the dealership and receive a check for a slightly lesser amount. “It's a win/win for everyone," said Bob. As I was driving home, I was thinking that Ms. Ross may just win the lottery one day! Nothing surprises me about Ms. Ross.

Over dinner, I was spreading the news to Marcus and the kids about Ms. Ross winning the minivan. They were all joking and hoping that I would win something really big soon. Maybe I will someday. I am thankful for winning the trip.

Later that night, I asked Marcus if he would be interested in going on the cruise with me. Marcus wanted to know when is the trip, where are we going, how are we going to get there, and how much is it going to cost him out of pocket. He sounded way too serious. I was beginning to feel like I was being cross examined by Perry Mason. I immediately turned over on my right side in bed, with my back facing Marcus. Before I switched the lamp to the off position, I said," ALL EXPENSES PAID!" I could hear Marcus trying to hold back a sneaky laughter.

It was early June, and we were boarding the plane for a flight to the LAX airport in Los Angeles, California. Upon arrival we took a cab to the Norwegian Cruise Line. The itinerary for the cruise stated that we would visit the Port of Los Angeles, Catalina Island and Ensenada, Mexico while cruising around the Pacific Ocean aboard the M/S Southward. The embarkation day has finally arrived!

As Marcus and I were boarding the ship, we had the opportunity to view the faces of many of the passengers that were exiting the ship. I will never forget that look on their faces because they looked really sad. This was not what I expected. Marcus boarded the ship with a smile. The ship did not set sail until sometime later. I was finally feeling enthusiastic about the trip. Marcus and Vera Henson were going on a cruise. I couldn't wait to see what our cabin would look like.

So far everything was going well. The kids were with my mom. The plane ride was great. Neither of us had ever flown before. We arrived safely in California. What could go wrong? The ship was huge, and the crew members were very friendly. Upon arriving at our assigned cabin, we were introduced to our first surprise. The cabin was sort of small and the sleeping arrangements were very peculiar. There were two twin beds, one on each side of the cabin. There was just enough room to store our luggage. I opened the door to the cabin's bathroom, and I decided right then and there that we were going to work with these accommodations. After all, how much time do you spend in the bathroom on a cruise ship?

Marcus and I were both looking forward to exploring the new surroundings. We both decided to have a drink. Drinking was sort of out of character for us because we only had one or two alcoholic beverages during the holidays. We went to the bar. Marcus ordered a beer, and I requested a glass of red wine. We found out very quickly that the drinks were not free. We will be drinking nonalcoholic beverages for the duration of the trip. Just as I was finishing up my one and only glass of wine, the ship had begun to sail.

Shortly thereafter, I immediately began to feel nauseated. I had never experienced this type of nausea before. My whole body was a bit off balance, and I just wanted to vomit. Maybe the wine was the culprit causing these symptoms. I was headed for a full-blown panic attack, until one of the crew members stepped in and took total control of my situation. I was escorted to a nearby table and chair. The crew member asked me several questions which I could not answer. Marcus provided most of the answers for me. It appears that I have developed motion sickness which is better known as seasickness.

Thank God I had purchased some Dramamine at the pharmacy a few days before the trip. I purchased the

Dramamine for Marcus, but Marcus was doing just fine. I reached into my handbag and retrieved the medication for motion sickness. While I was reading the directions on the bottle, the crew member walked over to the bar and returned with a glass of water. Within an hour, I had started to feel somewhat better, but now I was feeling a little drowsy, but the pills were working. I did not have any intentions of making a visit to the cruise ship's nursing staff.

Marcus remained cool and calm throughout my entire episode. Now that I was beginning to feel like myself again, I decided to return to the cabin to take a nap. Marcus settled for lounging out on the deck. It has been some time since he was able to relax and have a smoke.

There was a note on one of the beds that was left by a crew member. The message was for my attention only. I was congratulated on being a prize winner, and there was some verbiage about paying fees for port charges, which were not included in the all-expenses paid trip. The port charges were set at twenty-five dollars per port, per person. This was the $150.00 surprise! It was definitely time to take a nap.

Sometime later, after I had awakened from a refreshing nap, I could hear Marcus slightly snoring in the other bed. This was a great opportunity for me to pay the fees for the port charges. I didn't want Marcus to know anything about the extra expenses while we were together on the cruise ship. Both of us really needed a vacation and some time alone with each other. I am determined to stay positive, and hopefully there were no more surprises. After paying the necessary port charges, I returned to my cabin. Marcus was awakened by another crew member with a different message. I had forgotten about the assigned seating for the dining room. Dinner was being served in thirty minutes and we should arrive on time. We also had the privilege to attend a late-night setting, but we both knew that we would opt out.

Finding our way to the dining room was a no-brainer. You simply follow the crowd. Marcus reminded me to take my motion sickness drugs in a timely manner. I started with a twelve pack of Dramamine, and it appears that I may need all of them before the cruise ends. The dining room on the cruise ship was spectacular. It was beautiful and I had never seen anything so elegant. The lights appeared to be shining radiantly upon all of the guests as they were being seated at the tables. This was going to be an awesome experience and I was ready for it.

Our assigned table, which was beautifully decorated, had a seating set for ten people. Per my understanding, Marcus and I would share most meals in the main dining room with this same group of people. Maybe this was a great way for the passengers to assist the cruise line in keeping up with one another. Most of the guests at our table did not speak English, although they were very friendly.

A four-course meal was being served tonight. Marcus and I were looking forward to the prime rib, served with gravy covered mashed potatoes. There was a variety of food being served this evening, but this was not a buffet. The waiter, Martin, was very skilled in taking our orders and serving all of us in a timely manner. The meal was delicious, although I did not see many of the guests at our table blessing their meal prior to eating. Blessing our food is a routine for Marcus and I. We are not about to travel over fifteen hundred miles and lose ourselves on a cruise ship.

During dinner, Marcus moved a little closer to me to whisper something in my ear. "Don't eat too much of that bread and butter," says Marcus. I had to laugh at his joke, which was funny. We both had heard rumors over the years about overeating on cruise ships. Marcus knew that I was definitely not planning to put on any extra weight. So when our waiter asked if we needed any fresh bread, the answer was NO.

After dinner, we went sightseeing aboard the ship. There were lots of activities going on. We saw a small crowd of people gathering close to the casino entrance. The casino would open shortly after the ship entered a certain area of the ocean. My motion sickness pills were still working, so we decided to play the slot machines with a budget of thirty dollars each. Of course, this was also funny because we are not gamblers, and we don't have much money to lose.

Marcus walked over to my machine and asked, "Are you having any luck?" "Not yet", I replied. Marcus smiled and continued walking over to the last machine at the end of the aisle. Staying within my thirty dollar budget, I was finally down to my last ten dollars. I accidentally pressed the wrong button which cost me five dollars for one spin. I was determined that since I only have five more dollars to spin, I would spend it all and call it a night. You will never guess what happened next. I won a jackpot.

The slot machine started to make a lot of noise and the red light on top of the machine was flashing brightly. There were at least a dozen people standing way too close to me cheering louder than the slot machine. I was rescued by a floor attendant, who opened the machine to verify that I was indeed a winner. The attendant asked me to follow him to the cashier's office. At the cashier's office, I was asked to provide my identification. The cashier promptly counted out ten, one-hundred-dollar bills. I thought I was going to faint. This was a good surprise, but why did I feel like I was on a roller coaster ride at the fair? I asked the cashier to break one of the bills into ten-dollar bills, so that I could provide her and the attendant with a small tip. I placed the bills deep into the bottom of my handbag.

I spotted Marcus walking towards me, grinning all the way. "We are really having a good time tonight, Vera," said Marcus. "Yes, we are", I replied. "I managed to stay within the thirty-dollar budget, and I think that I am ready for bed", I said. Marcus decided to stay at the casino a little longer. Maybe he will have some good luck tonight too.

I returned to the cabin, and for the first time, I noticed that we had a small ocean view window. I walked over to the window to take a peep. There wasn't any land in sight or maybe my eyes were deceiving me. I also noticed that someone has freshly remade the beds and left some chocolate candy on both beds. Marcus will love this. Shortly after entering the shower, I heard the cabin door open and close. I am praying that it is Marcus because when I exit the bathroom, I don't want any surprises. I have already endured enough drama for today.

Marcus was sitting on his bed and attempting to take off the remaining one shoe. Our eyes did not meet until I slid over and proceeded to get into my bed, which was on the right side of the cabin. He was sporting a smile as usual. I could tell that he was in a really good mood. He was waiting for me to ask how much he won at the casino tonight. He continued to undress and kept his eyes on me the whole time. It was sort of romantic until Marcus tripped over his own shoes and landed at the door of the bathroom. "I still have moves", shouted Marcus on his way to the shower!

The following morning, we grabbed some breakfast and hurried to get in line for the offboarding at Catalina Island. We did not take the time to make the beds before leaving the cabin because the crew members made the beds almost every time we left the room. There were several older adults gearing up to go scuba diving. We declined the offer since scuba diving was not on our bucket list. I was delighted to be on land again and was ready for new sights to see. Marcus and I spent a great portion of our day relaxing at the beach. We had lunch at one of the restaurants near a small village which mostly served seafood. The scenery was beautiful. There were many large and small boats floating near Catalina Island. We saw many tall trees and small mountains made of rocks. We did not notice any cars on Catalina Island, only a few golf cart drivers. There are only two ways to get to Catalina Island. You must travel by sea or by air. It is the perfect place to get away! Hopefully we will return one day.

After returning to the ship, it wasn't long before I started to feel nauseous again. My body became very sensitive to the ship's departures. This time I was prepared, and I did not make a scene. I was able to locate a spot on the ship that was more soothing for my stomach than the inside of my cabin. There were a lot of activities happening on the ship tonight. The movie theater was crowded, so I didn't get the opportunity to see what was showing tonight. There were a few people working out in the exercise room even while on vacation. The pool held its share of visitors, and it looked like everyone was having a great time.

Marcus motioned for me to take a look into a contest that was being held aboard the ship. The grand prize was one thousand dollars. I immediately signed us up for this adventure! The contest starts in twenty minutes. Marcus and I both were so nervous. We have just entered a contest that we knew nothing about. "Let the fun begin," I said. There was a total of twenty-five contestants trying to win the contest. A theme song would be played from ten or more television shows and all that you have to do is provide the name of the show that matches the theme song. Almost everyone had the correct answer for the first few shows. *Bonanza* was number one, *Pink Panther* was number two, and *Rawhide* was number three. By the time the ninth theme song was played, there were only two contestants that were still active in the contest. That would be myself and a sweet, little old lady from Lake Tahoe. She had officially won the contest. The answer to the theme song was - *The Green Hornet*. I had no memory of the show whatsoever, but I had an awesome time.

The next day, we were offboarding to the Port of Ensenada, Mexico. We decided to splurge a little and go on a private bus tour. I had forgotten my disposable camera yesterday and was unable to take any pictures. Today, I was ready. I had heard so much about the blowhole, and I wanted to see it for myself. Marcus and I were the last two tourists to get off the bus. We had to walk some distance before we reached the area where the blowhole was located.

Along the way, we met several young children under the age of ten. They were walking right along beside us, and they spoke English fairly well. All of the children had some type of yarn and other crafting items. The youngest of the group asked me my name and I replied, "My name is Vera." He also asked me to spell my name and I replied, "V E R A". As we continued on our journey to the blowhole, for the time being, the little boy was making a bracelet. Upon completion of the beautiful bracelet, with my name hand weaved on the bracelet, the little boy asked if I liked the bracelet. The hand-crafted red and green bracelet was indeed a jewel, and it only cost me three dollars. I gave the little entrepreneur five dollars, and I did not expect any change. He was very thankful.

We made it to the blowhole and

there was a small crowd forming. The tour guide was very knowledgeable and provided answers to the tourists in English and Spanish. Several of us, including Marcus, climbed over a mountain of rocks and stones to get a view of the water movements. The tour guide stated that when the blowhole erupts, water could spray and reach the height of tall buildings. It appears that the blowhole has decided to take the day off. We did not witness this spectacular event today, but we will enjoy the view of the ocean.

After we boarded the bus, our next stop would be to have lunch and to do some shopping at the nearby local villages. There were tons of Mexican handicrafts and margaritas were being sold almost everywhere. I purchased a unique handmade blanket. The blanket is black and white, with an added smoky grayish color. I would love to buy more as souvenirs for the family, but there was not enough room in our luggage to accommodate any large items.

We did a lot of walking in Ensenada and truly enjoyed the scenery. As the bus was headed back to our drop off location, the tour guide continued to share with us more facts about Ensenada, Mexico. It seems that an individual could live very comfortably in Ensenada with an income of twenty-five thousand dollars. Now I began to understand why the little children were creating and selling bracelets in the community. We have so much to be thankful for.

Tonight, there was an eventful gathering in the main dining room. We were required to dress in formal attire. Marcus did not own a tuxedo and I did not have a cocktail dress, but we did look rather stunning in our attire. Marcus was dressed in a black suit and tie with his favorite charcoal black Stacy Adams. I was glowing in my carmine-colored dress with a side split that was exposing just a little too much of my thigh, but Marcus loved this dress. I put on my pearl necklace and the matching unpierced earrings that my mom gave to me last Christmas.

Most of the passengers had arrived early for the event and had already taken their assigned seats. Tonight, by far, was the best presentation ever. I was mesmerized by the beauty of the ice sculptures. They were delicately carved by a professional. The sculptures were large in size, and I really would have enjoyed watching the actual ice carvings of the butterfly and the swan.

It has to be sinful to devour this delicious meal. I have not taken the time to count any calories while aboard the cruise ship. The steak was prepared as ordered and the baked potato was magnificent. Marcus was enjoying a complete seafood dish and we both were making room for dessert. Marcus was going to take care of the gratuities for tonight. This was a moment that I shall never forget.

Tonight will be our last night aboard the ship. I am disappointed because I am not ready to leave. Even though the motion sickness was overwhelming I did survive. The atmosphere was very much needed, and I had some time to relax and think about a few things. Marcus and I both had a great time and hopefully we can go cruising again.

The following day as we were exiting the ship, I tried my best to put on a smiley face, but I just couldn't make it happen. So I looked down towards my feet instead of facing the newcomers. We received another surprise prior to offboarding. Someone had taken several photos of Marcus and I throughout the trip and they were available to purchase. How awesome is that? I could not believe my ears when Marcus agreed to purchase all of the photos.

Marcus and I hurried to take a cab back to LAX airport so that we would have plenty of time to check in and get the luggage put aboard the plane prior to departure. The cab driver talked all the way to the airport, while driving the scenic route. Later that day, we took our seats aboard the plane as we were looking forward to the flight going home. I can hardly wait to see the kids and to tell Ms. Ross all about the trip. Who knows, I just may win another vacation sometime soon!

www.ingramcontent.com/pod-product-compliance
Lightning Source LLC
Chambersburg PA
CBHW070617310726
48982CB00001B/108

* 9 7 8 1 6 3 9 6 0 0 3 1 1 *